Selected Short Stories

of

Dónall MacAmhlaigh

An Irish Community Arts Project

Compiled selection
first published 2001
by Northampton Connolly Association
5 Woodland Avenue, Abington
Northampton NN3 2BY

An Irish Community Arts Project

British Library Cataloguing in Publication Data
MacAmhlaigh, Dónall
Selected Short Stories of Dónall MacAmhlaigh
Title
Author
Irish Diaspora
Irish in Britain

823.914 [F]
ISBN O-9510671-1-7

Distributed by
The Four Provinces Bookshop
244 Gray's Inn Road
London WC1X 8JR

Typeset in Times 11 point by The Irish Community Arts Project

Printed by
Pickards Colour Publishing
Sheffield

Contents

INTRODUCTION 5

1. MILLESVILLE - A WORKER REMINISCES 7

2. POETS AND POTTINESS 11

3. TALK AND EMIGRATION 15

4. CHAPTER AS IN BOOK 19

5. A HAIRSHIRT FOR MARY HORAN 23

6. POET, PROFESSOR AND GENIUS 27

7. THE STORY OF MR BARKER 33

8. TALKING TO THE BBC 37

9. NOT LONG FOR LAING 41

10. RETURN TO DUBLIN 45

11. THE CRACK 49

12. KIT'S STORY 57

13. THE WORKS 63

14. SWEENEY 83

15. DÓNALL PEADAR MAC AMHLAIGH 91

Introduction

The last three decades has, for the Irish in Britain, been a time of growing up. In that period a generation has lived in digs, built the railways, the motorway and the underground; and in the process created a unique history of a Diaspora by adding another sub-culture to the mainstream British culture. That sub-culture fed on the fact, fiction and myths of a previous generation of Irish workers in Britain. The fact that the work we did was hard and the working conditions often cruel. The fiction that the garden was greener in Britain and there was big money to be made by working even harder for those who we knew were exploiting us; and the myth that our working lives here were transient and we would all return, in the due course of time, to Ireland, richer and wiser. We did not return - we married and settled here. Our children were born here. Here became our home. But we kept up our connection with our homeland. In some cases that connection was strong. In others it was tenuous. But even if the latter was the case it was fast becoming obvious that we were still Irish and our children were Irish and we, and they, could not be anything else. This reaffirmation of identity was something that we did not, in most cases, deliberately set out to foster. It was in fact created by a larger framework of political circumstances, one of which was the resistance to British rule in Northern Ireland. Even more so this new found identity was created by Britain's reaction to that resistance in Ireland and the propaganda of war against Ireland and the now identified Irish community in Britain. Referred to as the 'enemy within' by one conservative politician. This was the main factor that caused us to step back from assimilation. The host culture was antagonistic to Irish aspirations. In the face of Britain's propaganda war against the Irish, which often took a racialist form, we had to decide where we stood. But we could not stand alone. We required a distinctive individual identity, a distinctive culture and more so a distinctive community that could easily be identified. We got all three with the help of the British media whose ability to berate and denigrate us rose and fell with the intensity of the war in Northern Ireland.

We are now a distinctive community with our own history, culture and newspapers. Our political awareness, as a community, is growing fast. We are here to stay. It is the history of our community that we are concerned with here and one man, among a few, stands out as a recorder of the Irish experience in Britain. Dónall MacAmhlaigh was born in Galway but most of his working life was spent in Britain. He worked on all the major building sites in the East Midlands from Milton Keynes to the M6. His working life was typical of the genre and as such he was ideally suited to reflect the trials and tribulations of the immigrant. His writings give us a sense of history, a sense of belonging, of being near Ireland physically, culturally and in spirit, but yet of living in Britain with all that that entails. Dónall expressed through the medium of his books and short stories the trauma of leaving and the experience of surviving in a strange culture whose values were often quite different from what we knew or expected. Dónall recognised these values and cultures - where they met and where they clashed is the raw material of his stories. Dónall, or Danny as he was called locally, died in Northampton in 1989. The secretary accepts responsibility for the selection of the stories published here. They were all taken from original material submitted to the Irish Democrat and are reproduced by kind permission of the directors of Connolly Publications Ltd.

Financial assistance received from The Ireland Fund made the production of this publication possible.

Peter Mulligan
Secretary,
Northampton Connolly Association

Chapter One

MILLSVILLE - A WORKER REMINISCES

I began work forty six years ago next month; the pay was eleven shillings (55p) a week - a 35 hour week until I reached the age of seventeen some twelve months later - plus a monthly discretionary bonus of £2.00, a sort of wartime arrangement, if my memory serves me right, to get around a government policy of pay restrictions. The bonus was conditional on good time keeping and behaviour and it was rarely that anyone failed to get it but it made a tremendous difference and brought my weekly average to a guinea a week, a substantial sum in a working class home in 1943. The hours certainly were not excessive when you consider the moves afoot here in Britain now to take off the restrictions on juveniles working long hours; but some of the work was laborious enough. Leaving school at sixteen meant I had the benefit of two years more than most of the other lads of my age I worked with in the woollen mills, where I got my first job. Fourteen was the legal school leaving age then and in consequence of my extra time at the Christian Brothers School, I was accorded a totally undeserved regard as a 'brainy chap'. In fact due to our moving about the county quite a bit I had been at a number of schools and lost out in the process so that I was a year older than everyone else in my class in Kilkenny.

I did not stay on for the Intermediate Certificate - roughly the equivalent of the British 'O' levels exams I believe - for the simple reason that I couldn't afford to. The few shilling being very much needed at home, but as a product of the C.B.S. and the kind of thinking so prevalent in Ireland at the time, I aspired to rather grander things than a labouring job at the mills. I had taken a commercial course at the Brothers and was well versed in the art of writing sycophantic letters to employers, declaring my many excellent qualities as a prospective employee and swearing ceaseless loyalty and diligence in my work to whichever employer might see fit to give me a trial. It didn't avail me anything; a succession of applications for office jobs brought polite refusals at best and even a job behind a counter was very hard to come by in those days. Just before I managed to get the mill job I had tried for a job as messenger boy - delivering groceries on a heavy bike with a wicker basket out front - and luckily failed. I hurried home with the news of my success the day I got taken on in the mills with a kind of elation I haven't experienced too often since. My first job in the woollen mills was that of a waste wool sorter, separating two or three grades of the waste product that varied from fairly-usable carded wool (for export and reuse in Britain) to junk fit only for the tip, broken pieces of metal, wooden perrins damaged beyond use and so forth. It wasn't the kind of job that makes any great demands on the intellect, infact, the greatest *'amadan'* who ever drew breath could do it but there was a slight or perhaps not so slight complication; I was in the throes of a long-vanished ailment at the time, a kind of mild lunacy known as religious scruples. Most people, I imagine, won't have a notion of what I am talking about now but it was a common enough phenomenon at the time among Catholic youngsters, a preoccupation with sin, especially with sins relating to the temptations of the flesh, which could assume the most alarming proportions. To put it in a nutshell victims of religious scruples went through a kind of perpetual torment imagining that almost everything they did and said was a sin. Harassed confessors were known to dread having to hear confessions of scruple victims who were largely convinced that their wickedness was irremediable and that the poor unfortunate man hearing their confessions had no grasp at all of the extent of their iniquities. It would not have been so bad in my case if my scruples had confined themselves to sexual matters and the kind of temptations which a lop-sided biology put in the way of youngsters with no means of utilising their urges and too often deny to adults who have every opportunity. No, my scruples weren't content with that, they had to invade the workplace and interfere with my judgment as to what was and what was not first-class waste. In consequence of this I used to agonise over every fistful of the filthy stuff, dithering like a faint-hearted, would-be-suicide on the edge of a precipice - should I put the 'glaum' of hairy, oily, gritty waste in the 'best' basket or the other one? Needles to say my production was almost nil for a time until in the end I had aroused the understandable suspicions of the management that I was sleeping a large part of my working day. I was given an ultimatum; do more work or vacate the job for a more diligent employee! Faced with that ultimatum and the impossibility of explaining to the Ma how I had come to lose so cushy a job I threw myself into the sorting with a kind of abandon that only a lifelong saint who had suddenly lost his belief in the next world would surrender himself to in an orgy of sin. My production certainly improved, indeed if you were to think of it in terms of those wall charts which industrialists use to describe the fortunes of their companies my output would be shown as a perpendicular rise going out of the top of the frame. This was less of a blessing to my employer than might at first be thought since he soon had an irate letter from some place in Bradford billing him for a couple of hundred pounds in respect of damage sustained by machinery into which all the junk, bits of wood and metal and what have you ensconced in the waste wool was fed. The Bossman solemnly informed me across the top of his office desk that he'd be quite within his legal rights in billing me for the money demanded over in Bradford and stopping it at so much a week from my pay. Even paying it back, interest free, I imagine I'd have been well into maturity before the debt was cleared. But thankfully he opted for another course and transferred me to the wool-sorting department proper where I was entrusted with the even less dignified task of snipping hardened blobs of sheep dung (or dog ends as they were properly called) from fleeces which the wool-sorters tore into about five different categories, a category to each basket. These men worked at an incredible speed and with a highly developed tactile sense so that they need not look the fleeces they were ripping apart at all, they could tell just from the feel what grade or quality they had in hand. Moonlighting was a rare enough thing in those days of scarce employment but we had two men in the woollen mills who augmented their wages with a second job. One of them was the boilerman who manually fed the furnace that powered the steam mill, a Herculean task that involved shovelling coal, turf and sticks into the glowing maw of the boiler. He washed his hands at night though God along knows how he managed to get them sufficiently clean, donned a black waiter's suit, white front and dicky bow, and waited on tables at the Club House Hotel or whatever else his services were required; I have always thought that there should have been a medal or system of honours of some sort for such dedication to hard work (or money - or whatever!). The other moonlighter was a wool sorter and he doubled at night, perhaps three nights a week as a drummer in a dance band. He was the most expert of the sorters with an output that meant he could afford to slip away for a few hours and burrow deep into a pile of fleece to make up for the sleep he lost the night before as an entertainer. It was my job to go and wake him at an appointed time, or earlier if there was any fear of his absence being noted. I performed this function with considerable diligence but often as not my thanks was a sleepily order to 'Feck off with yourself and leave me alone'.

ID 1-MCMLXXX1X

Chapter Two

MILLSVILLE - POETS AND POTTINESS

Wool workers in the Greenvale Woollen Mills where I worked enjoyed a considerable status and they were forever telling the rest of us how much in demand they - or their skills - were in Australia; not that any of them had the slightest intention of going there! And for all that they were on piece rates and worked with deft speed, they never had any of what is called 'hassle' nowadays about their wages, whereas the weavers were forever besieging the office, irate and indignant because they had been underpaid. No doubt it was more difficult to work out the weavers' output but they too were highly valued and on occasion they displayed a degree of militancy, which few of us unskilled hands would attempt. There was plenty of banter and backchat in the wool sorting area, a constant slagging competition between the drummer whom it was my job to wake in the afternoon if he had been playing at a dance somewhere the night before. The drummer who was called Harry Tunstall (a very English name but of course English names are as common among the Irish as Irish names are among the English) was all for the modern life - what was then regarded by many as decadent foreign music - the big band thing - whereas his antagonist; a countryman called Martin Dowling, was a fervent nationalist in a sentimental and uncritical way. Martin knew perhaps a couple of dozen phrases in Irish and he never failed to practice them on me; this provoked Harry T to immense amusement and he would respond with catch phrases like 'Ta se mahogany gaspipe! (Wogan fans will be familiar with that one!) or some other such nonsense. This in turn provoked charges of Anglophilia - though in less polite language - from Martin and sincere protestations of his own unswerving devotion to Ireland. Looking back at it now it amazes me how much opposition there was to what was loosely termed 'jazz' in those days. When I was at school some teacher or other was forever denigrating 'jungle music' which of course it was not at all. But I suppose that kind of intolerance must be the natural outcome of cultural deprivation, among those sensitive enough to be aware of their cultural deprivation anyway, because there is no need for it where people do not feel culturally threatened. I have always found more anti-Britishness among the more Anglicised townsfolk of Kilkenny than in Irish-speaking Connemara. I had begun at this time to acquire something of a reputation as a local poet, God help us! There were a number of such in every Irish town and maybe parish at the time, chaps and girls who got their outpourings printed in the local paper, but not of course paid for, no editor would be that daft! and who enjoyed quite a high regard in consequence. Some poets wrote in the well-established traditional ballad mode and thus couldn't go very far within the limits of the form and their own very limited ability. But I was more influenced by Palgrav's 'Golden Treasury of English Verse' and some of my efforts were very highfalutin - and far more nonsensical than the honest pedestrian work of the mainly rural poets, most of whose compositions began with lines like "I recall as once I wandered" or "One evening fair to take the air as out I chance to stray." Originality was never valued too highly by these versifiers and the fact that someone - or more likely some hundred other poetasters - had written more or less the same lines didn't bother them at all. I smugly despised all such modest aspirations and instead plagiarised the works of the mighty; an example might not come amiss here and those who know that immortal poem by Thomas Gray 'Elegy in a Country Churchyard' will note some faint and ludicrous echoes of it in the following which I was inordinately proud of at the time.

'The fishermen with patient rod and line

Along the darkling riverbank await

The ripple, rug or well-interpre'd sign

Rewarding a judicious choice of bait.'

Poets, be they the real McCoy or deluded poor rhymers, are a very jealous breed and though we sometimes praised each other's work to each other's faces we never believed the kind words that we spoke and indeed we sometimes attacked each other quite intemperately in print. One chap had what I considered the temerity to attack my verse, but anonymously, in the Kilkenny People and I immediately responded with the following charming lines:

'You village wit, you tap-room poet,

you feeble-minded creature,

Why sir, you dare not pen your name

to that ill favoured feature!'

The editor may have been a very tolerant and patient man but needless to say he drew the line at publishing that kind of vitriol! The odd thing though is that however facile and worthless the kind of verse I wrote then, I think that I'd have my work cut out to manage it now; its a kind of a knack - however useless! - I suppose, that one loses as soon as a modicum of critical gumption is gained.

Harry the woolsorter was the very first workingman to the best of my knowledge who became the proud possessor of a motorcar in Kilkenny - certainly in the woollen mills. The car became something of a necessity if he was to keep up with his dance-band commitments round the country but he sometimes drove it to work, especially if he was late in the morning which he often was (the mills were situated over a mile from the city). Harry's arrival in Greenvale in an old Ford caused a share of talk and amusement and I quickly seized on the event to compose a little verse to mark the occasion. I can't remember more than the odd snatch of it now but the burden of the thing was that the bold Harry set up new records for speed and recklessness, causing havoc on the way:

'A bonamh, a duck and a sheepdog
lay stretched in our Harry's wild wake
but nothing impeded the speed hog
continued all records to break........'

A bonamh for the benefit of anyone who may not know is the Irish word for a piglet.

I was not the only "poet" in the mills. There was a challenge to my position from a chap who worked in the dye pots, a sturdy youngster who I think later died in Korea, and he was even more lacking in gumption than myself, if such a thing was possible. Ricky, as I'll call him, conceived the notion of writing a poem about our place of work and having written it he marched from his work place straight up to the office - rather in the manner of Mad McGonagle the Scottish poet when he called to see Queen Victoria, unasked at Balmoral or wherever it was - and likewise Ricky asked if he could speak with the Boss! The Boss, a formidable character, a real eccentric given to the most unwarranted expressions of favour and ill-favour, quite despotic in some ways and very benevolent in others, granted an interview and asked Ricky what his business was. Ricky proudly informed the Boss that he had just written a poem about the mills and would like to recite it there and then for him - I kid not, so help me God! "Proceed," the Boss told him and Ricky proceeded. I knew the whole rubbishy farrago of nonsense by heart at the time and derived a great deal of malicious pleasure from reciting it to others; all I recall of it now is the first stanza that went as follows;

'As I was travelling in Kilkenny
I found things far from still
I heard the sound of a hooter
I knew 'twas the Greenvale Mill...'

There were some five verses in all, concluding with the odd information that the poet would refrain from naming those employed in the mill because 'they are valiant and true!'

The Boss heard Ricky out and then he showed him out with the rather unappreciative remark that he would dock the appropriate amount of wages in respect of the time spent away from his work! This show of philistinism didn't deter Ricky and he continued to compose poems for quite some time after.

ID 11-MCMLXXX1X

Chapter Three

TALK AND EMIGRATION

People talk a lot about the trauma of emigration, and alienation. I suppose if you came to industrial Britain from the heart of rural Ireland thirty or forty years ago, before the age of television, you might experience something like that. But I was town-bred, partly at least, and I was familiar with the outside world if only through the cinema. Also I read a lot, so I didn't think or feel I was coming to anywhere terribly foreign or strange when I came to England.

I was lonely to be sure, heartsick with longing for home many's the time, but there was nothing like trauma or alienation as there might have been if I'd come straight from the heart of Connemara where the people had a pure Irish/Gaelic culture undiluted by any of the influences of the English-speaking world. In my case there was an odd sense of having been here before, what the French call déjà vu. We worked awkward split shifts in the hospital, you might be free from nine in the morning till half twelve in the afternoon and then work on till eight o'clock in the evening or you might be off one to five - I used to walk a lot in my spare time. I'd ramble off out the road past the little shopping area and the White Hills pub, the rows of semi-detached houses, and it used to seem to me that I had been here before. I suppose if you're exposed to the influence of another country from the time you learn to read, if the bulk of your reading material comes from such a country as well as a lot of the films you see, then naturally, enough you will be familiar with it, you will even feel a certain affinity with it. Cultural domination is what some people call it, the influence that England, the English language and its literature have had on the Irish and it all began a very long time ago. Where the tongue is English the heart must be English too, old Henry the Eight said when he set out to anglicise the Irish. You could argue with that contention I suppose but there is a lot in it too - how English would the English themselves be, if some other country had imposed its language on them?

At any rate I didn't feel I had come to any place very strange to me, or foreign, though there were a lot of things about the English that rather threw me - the forthright way so many of them had of asking you something that an Irishman would beat round the bush to find out; it's a kind of honesty I suppose that we don't have, not in the same way at least. The English sense of humour was another thing that left me cold... I mean I read P.G.

Wodehouse and the likes, I could laugh my head off at Jeeves and Bertie Wooster and later on I could enjoy the humour of Evelyn Waugh; but a lot of the everyday English humour I heard around me didn't amuse me at all. I mean, a funny dirty story is a funny dirty story in any language but a lot of what I'd call lavatory humour - the jokes that comedians tell on radio or television - I couldn't find funny at all. What I'm trying to say is that for all my familiarity with England and English through reading and the cinema, for all that their language was my language and my language was theirs I often felt that there was a great gulf between us. This was more apparent, I think, in the pub than anywhere else; the English, it seemed to me, were people of 'measured merriment'- to borrow a turn of phrase from Sinclair Lewis. The English pub seemed to me a particularly dull environment and the fondness for pub games - darts, skittles, dominoes and the rest irritated me. The drink seemed to be only a secondary consideration, you rarely, it seemed to me, heard anyone say appreciatively, as they might do over a pint of Guinness in Dublin, "Janey but that's a great blooming' pint". I think English society has changed a lot over the years; it has become a lot more violent. When I came over here first the Irish were a bye-word for fighting and brawling - a cause of serious scandal to the native population we were often told by the priests - but in truth it was pretty harmless violence compared with much of what you have today - two aging Paddies, it might be, swapping wild punches outside the boozer at closing time; or a couple of younger chaps at the Irish dance throwing their jackets off to fight.

It gave the local folk plenty to talk about and there was plenty of talk, but of course what's rare is wonderful as they say in Irish, and by and large there wasn't much brawling or violence of that nature among the native population then, not in this part of the Midlands anyway and not as far as I observed in other areas either. The English by and large struck me, when I came here to work, first as a very gentle people - well, you could differ from them in an argument, you could even throw history at them and remind them of all they did wrong in Ireland and you weren't in danger of getting a belt in the gob as they say! I'd rather argue the toss with an Englishman any day than with other nationalities I could mention, including some of my own. Just the same as there is a degree of violence among the young men of today here in England that would have amazed their fathers and grandfathers thirty of forty years ago. They are far less temperate, too, in the matter of drink, the youngsters guzzle pints of lager as well as any of the old-time navvies guzzled beer.

The old Irish stereotype of the boozy, brawling Paddy began to fade away I think at the time when emigration from Ireland had slowed to a trickle - in the early 1970's when in fact there was a reversal and more people returned to take up work in the Republic than left there, well, you got the impression of the Irish here in Britain - certainly in this part of the Midlands - as an aging population, they weren't then being replaced by youngsters over from Ireland because there was near full employment there. I remember talking to English brickies in Limerick in 1970 and being told by them that they were getting more per thousand bricks there in Limerick than in the new city of Milton Keynes... the stereotype of the Irishman in Britain underwent a certain change and this was more and more reflected in the 'Irish joke' and the kind of patter television comedians came out with, the Irishman was more and more being depicted as a down at heel, aging buffoon - a version of the many unfortunates, alcoholics or derelicts you may see in any major town in Britain, the kind of people who couldn't adapt very well to Thatcher's Britain ... A lot of us objected to the old stereotype, the big rough labourer, boozy and quarrelsome. But like all the Irish who had traditionally filled the role of unskilled labour in Britain, by the very nature of things the unskilled labourer will be a rough and ready person. What the English saw in the 1950s was an influx of mainly rural Irish who played a disproportionately high role in construction work - if you saw a brawny chap waist-deep in a hole on the side of the road it was a fair bet he was Irish and if the same fellow cut loose at the weekend in the boozer then it wasn't an altogether unreasonable assumption for the native to make that Paddy was an intemperate, rough diamond... that such a character might only represent a minority of Irish was neither here nor there.

ID VI-MCMLXXXVIII

Chapter Four

CHAPTER AS IN BOOK

CHAPTER was the nickname an old ganger on the East Midlands Electricity Board gave me - that was in the summer of 1959. I always brought a book to work with me and I'd read a bit of it during the dinner break - we had an hour for dinner on the Board, not a skimped half hour like you'd get on the building. I left the building that summer to take a job on the Electricity Board; took a cut in money too, but you were finished nice and early every day and I needed the time. I was writing you see, and I had started on a book early that summer. The old ganger's name was Smithy - nicknamed Punch - a real character he was and a typical old-time soldier. He'd had the distinction, if that's the right word, of being the last British soldier to leave the Curragh Camp in Co. Kildare in 1922. One day he brought out an old faded page of the Daily Mirror and there he was in his full marching order, puttee and black webbing, tin hat and Lee Enfield rifle, and a corgi dog under each arm! Through some cock-up Punch had been left on guard duty at the water tower - a high brick building in the Curragh - after all his comrades had been relieved by the new Free State troops. These couple of corgi dogs belonging to some British officer had been left behind too, and poor old Punch got lumbered with them!

Punch wasn't too keen on the reading business, and any man that brought a book on the job couldn't have his mind on his work, Punch believed! Not that you'd need to go to Oxford or Cambridge to do the work we were on - all we had to do was dig so much trench out, it was all hand-work of course, pick and shovel or digging fork if you liked, and pull in the length of cable. It wasn't like private contractor's work where you'd be flat out, all go and maybe some Irish gangerman bawling at you to get moving, they were satisfied with a reasonable day's work on the Board and it was unionised too - the old ETU if I remember right, though I think you could opt for the TGWU if you liked. There was one chap on the job, he was an Irishman like myself, and he wouldn't belong to the ETU because it was communist controlled. That was the least of my objections; I've always been a socialist even if only a lazy one.

Punch never found fault with my work, though, whatever about labelling me 'Chapter.' I like manual unskilled work - as long as you're not killed of course, I'm not saying I'd want to be a lather of sweat all day or anything like that, but there's some thing very soothing in a bit of 'manual dig' as they call it to-day; or barrowing concrete, you get in a rhythm and it seems you could go on forever. And of course you know that your money is there assured at the end of the week not like the writing lark! A man might spend a fortnight toiling over a short story, writing and rewriting and revising and all that, and never even had it published. I began work early enough in life - just gone sixteen - and I'm all for the prospect of a regular wage. The funny thing about that - about the business of rewriting and revision - is that the first book I wrote, and the one that made most impact, that book was dashed off you might say in a couple of months, writing after my day's work of course, I couldn't afford to go at it full time. I was on the construction of the M1 then - oh, a very minor role indeed, sweeping up or humping road forms, there wasn't an awful lot of pick and shovel as such, the big cats and the grader did the muckshifting. I was on the bridges too for a spell, concreting - good bonus there - and scabbing, things like that. So the writing was done at night and I was drawing on old diaries I had kept since 1948.

I had an old Royal Standard typewriter at the time, it was as solid as a tank, you could drop it on the floor I'm sure and the floor would come off worse. We weren't long married at the time and the poor wife must have been demented, there in one small room, listening to the clacking of the typewriter keys. "Ah, you're clacking again," she'd sigh, "can't you leave it for one night?" I was lucky really to get a book published so easily at all, you see it came about by chance, really - an article I wrote in Irish for a magazine, just a piece based on some old diary extracts from the time I worked down in Norfolk, a place called Diss. That was in 1954, we were working for a company called ORMAC - short for O'Reilly-McLoughlin - it was all hand-dig down there, a mobile crane lowering skips that we filled with the shovels. Running sand, every inch of it, they had a dewatering plant in operation around the clock and you had to timber every foot of the cutting or it would be in on top of you, being sand. Well, I'd always wanted to write something and when I was just left school and working in the mills at home in Kilkenny I'd written this nonsensical, long rambling novel that no publisher in his right mind would look at. After that I did the odd sketch or short story and I used to contribute dreadful poems, the Lord save us, to the local papers - there were two of them then, believe it or not, in a small Irish town of eleven thousand! But I was married and into my early thirties before I got anything published to speak of - that was the article about our time down in East Anglia working for ORMAC and no sooner was it in print that I had this letter asking if I had much of that sort of material, enough to make a book maybe? Indeed I had, and enough for half a dozen books if it was worth printing. Well they told me to get cracking and I did, belting away night after night on the old Royal Standard, never rewriting a line or even reading back over what I had written, you see I hadn't a clue really about the business. We have a saying in Irish *'Námha an cheird gan a fhoghlaim'* - which doesn't translate readily but means more or less that the craftsman should know his craft - and I didn't! I missed a great opportunity there, I could have made a great book out of that if I had known the craft, things I could have elaborated on more, scenes and characters I might have developed better; I needn't have sacrificed *'truth'* to *'fact'* if you know what I mean. What the book had going for it was this: I was the first ordinary, you might well say *'uneducated'* working class Irishman to have written about the experience of being a labouring man in Britain - that is to say the first for a long time. Patrick McGill the Donegall navvy-poet as he was called, did it in fiction form to be sure - best selling novels like 'The Rate Pit' - and 'Children of the Dead End' - but that was in the first quarter of the present century; then there was a book called 'In a Strange Land' by John O'Donoghue an ex-Civic Guard who came over during the war years to work in Britain - Sean O'Faolain wrote a glowing preface to it by the way. But apart from the very odd thing here and there I had the field to myself and bad use I made of the advantage I'm sorry to say. I'm not saying the book wasn't well received, when it came out first in Irish in 1960 and a few years later when it appeared in English translation under the title of 'An Irish Navvy' I wouldn't have chosen that title myself, by the way, it seemed a mite boastful, a navvy to my mind being a mighty worker and I wouldn't put myself in that category at all. But that was the publishers idea, they knew best- if they did! The original was in Irish, as I say, I called it 'Dialann Deoraí - an exiles diary, because of course it was drawn from my old diaries which were very short and even cryptic in part.

I don't believe the Irish were ever really afflicted with the wanderlust, going all over the globe for the fun of it. There may have been a few such but the bulk of my generation that came over here to Britain came for the good and sufficient reason that they had no prospects of work at home, not worthwhile work at any rate, and there was bags of employment in England. "Any useless yoke at all can get a job in England," a publican's wife said to me in Kilkenny one day - I don't know whether she considered that I was in that category, a useless yoke, or not, but she marvelled that work could be had so easily across the water. I marvelled myself when I came here first, the vacancy columns were chocabloc with jobs and there was something for everybody; the educated and the uneducated alike, the weak and the strong, the skilled and the unskilled. My first job when I came here in 1951 was as a ward orderly in a hospital, it's closed now, the Government cut-backs. The Health Service was so short of staff in those days they had to advertise in the Irish papers, some hospitals paid your way over and there was accommodation awaiting you in the residential quarters, a big thing that, a big inducement to someone like myself arriving with little or no money and not in a position to pay for digs right off. It was the same with public transport, they'd send representatives over to the labour exchanges in Ireland with offers of work in London or Birmingham or wherever it was - building firms also recruited in this way. Many's the man who had done well for himself in construction, became a general foreman or an agent, or owning his own firm even, came across from Ireland on the old Princess Maud with McAlpine or a Wimpey label pinned to his coat.

ID 111-MCMLXXXV111

Chapter Five

A HAIR SHIRT FOR MARY HORAN

TOO GOOD, too soon, - the expression is one heard very often nowadays both on the lips of the Irish at home and on the lips of their compatriots here in Britain. What is meant by it is that the Republic grew prosperous too fast and somehow in consequence of this, must now go into a long period of poverty, or at least of that relative poverty which some of us, thirty or forty years ago, would have considered affluence. Like many popular sayings this one should be made to stand scrutiny to try and ascertain whether there is more than a grain of truth in it (there must be *'that'* much at least) or if it is just one of these 'clichès' which people parrot happily because that is easier to do than go through the - admittedly - hard process of thinking. I'm no great shakes at that process myself, so I know what I'm talking about. The assumption would seem to be that we - the majority - are not really entitled to a good going-on and that if we enjoy it for a period we must then go through a sort of purgatory of amendment until we have well and truly paid for our spell of affluence. I don't know what the appropriate name is for this theory but one exists, I don't doubt and certainly the vast majority of people seem to subscribe to it. Take for example the docility of the British worker today, when things are bad, as compared to a few years ago - when things were good. I commented on this recently in an article called ëOn the Lineí here in the Democrat and a friend and correspondent with a far better grasp of the socio-historical process than I have wrote to say that the workers were only conforming, in this, to the traditional pattern of behaviour. I must confess I was not aware that such a pattern had been established although in ordinary human terms it is perfectly understandable that it would. I have made this point before, time and again, the point being that human nature tends itself to take advantage of generosity and kindness and, child-like must be rebuked and restrained. Let me elaborate, a mild mannered and tolerant wife is generally taken for granted and even exploited by her husband - bua raicleach - as we say in Irish (a termagant in good Bearla!) often gets her own way and even puts the screws on the hubby...I heard a woman say once, "There was always Women's Liberation all they had to do was take it." It was certainly true in her case because the husband waits hand and foot on her, not I must hasten to add from love, but from a moral dread of her tongue and temper. The good lady in question drew a howl of laughter in the pub, once, when asked what she'd have to drink she replied "I'll have a large vodka please - and half a beer for himself!"

Similarly an employer - circumstances favouring - will work the genitals off a willing employee and pay him as little as possible; and circumstances being reversed no doubt the hard done employee would put the boot in 'old master' with equal enthusiasm! That would seem to be our natural bent and hitherto the most we expected of the Trade Union Movement was to counter the rapacity and unfairness of employers; I use the word 'hitherto' in a fairly loose way as for twenty years and more the Labour Party were enlisting the help of the Unions in holding back pay claims. A similar role would seem to be expected of the unions in socialist countries and who is to say that unions must forever remain a basically negative force merely exacting what they may for their members? I presume that if we had real socialism tomorrow, and if the unions still had a role, they would be expected to look for no more for members than the State could afford to pay them. Socialists I imagine would accept that, if not happily, at least with enlightened resignation. But when we are appealed to by employers, manufacturers and government people, who have very little intention of making sacrifices, to tighten our belts and brace ourselves for a long hard slog then we may be pardoned for not being as wholeheartedly co-operative as they might wish. In the Republic today people are being told that they have had it too good too soon and that they must now pay the price. If that is so then the price will no doubt be paid - but mainly by the wage earner I'll bet! Will land speculators or those professional people who have been revealed as shameless tax dodgers in the Republic make sacrifices willingly? I tend to doubt it.

Few cities, I mustn't say 'town' in this context because the people of Ye Faire Citie take exception to the word when used to describe their own bailiwick, fared so well or resisted the recession so long, as Kilkenny, but when it came, it came with a vengeance and the Labour Exchange is once more reminiscent of the bad old days of the 1950's when the unemployed queued in a long ragged line to sign on every day. Some publicans find that it is not worth their time opening at all now during the day (the pint was about 98p on average when I was home in October, and the position will be worse now, presumably with the latest increase of 2p). Surely the Law of Diminishing Returns must come into operation any day now and the Government will be faced with the realisation that they will gain less, not more, from the increase. The big difference between now and the Fifties is that there is no outlet to Britain. Nor does the younger generation evince any desire to go to Britain. That too is a big change. In fact a while generation with an entirely different outlook has grown up and the notion of having to go to another country as a matter of course to earn a living is quite foreign to them. But no country can hope to escape crime and civil unrest if it has nothing but idleness to offer an energetic young population and this Christmas has seen acts of lawlessness and violence almost unparalleled in the history of the State. These acts must - and will - be curbed and punished insofar as the authorities are capable of it, but the root cause will remain and the crime and lawlessness go on unless the country can offer some thing better than the dole to its young.

How is it that the quality which most of us perceive as Irishness can exist and even flourish out of Ireland, sometimes, more than in Ireland? I am thinking now of how very Irish in attitude, cultural preference and so forth so many of our people here in Britain seem to be by comparison with so many at home. Radio Eireann is for me a lifeline with Ireland but there is a whole world reflected therein the babbling of the commercial breaks which interrupt the programmes so frequently - that is as alien to people like myself as anything we might pick up on a European station hundreds of miles away. Who recruits the gibbering young men and women who bleat about the bargains at Quinnsworths, or croon that 'Milk's the one' from where do they get their half-American and more than half English accents? There must be a whole world in Ireland, which the likes of myself would shrink from as from the touch of an unfortunate leper. The beauty and integrity of being what you are - an Englishman who is true to himself, to his cultural upbringing, to all that has made him, be he an aristocrat or an labouring man, has a wholeness, an integrity, a naturalness that is to be admired and respected - but when you get an Irish person aping the tones of Portland Place or Yankeeland with an ersatz, of an accent you can only cringe with shame and embarrassment.

At least when a man is at home he can avoid such people and even on occasion almost convince himself that not too many of them exist. Kilkenny yielded the usual pleasures, the unaffected friendship and goodwill, the homely turn of speech, the unconquerable sense of humour, which sees the funny side of the blackest of situations. "Poor oul Butler is dead" said a countryman coming in for his pint to a well known Noreside hostelry, "I know, but wasn't he the lucky man - he got all his hay saved before he went," replied another. Or the one about the farmer, boasting in his cups that he "drank all ever he had." "Aye," replied his drinking companion, "and that wasn't a great deal!"

I could have stayed in Kilkenny but Galway and the Gealtacht called too and my time was all too short. The recession had hit Galway and points west, and a friend who had made some pretty shrewd prognostications in the past told me that he believed we'd see cars rusting behind the houses for want of the wherewithal to keep them on the road. The little Gealtacht factories are closing like nobody's business and if there was work in England no doubt a new generation of Gaeilgeoiri would be making for Dun Laoghaire and the Bad Ban. Still and all Connemara seems a good place to live; I found laughter and the crack there, a few pints being downed and the ready welcome which you value all the more long in a place that has little time to spare for such thing. Many of the things which preoccupy (obsess even) us here in Britain just don't seem to impinge very much on the consciousness of the Irish at home - whether this is a good or a bad thing I'm not sure. Living here in prime target area in the English Mid lands I frequently wonder - if I don't actually worry - about the likelihood of the Bomb - but somehow back in Coise Fharraige or in Derrynea things like that seem immeasurably remote. They seem, alas, for in truth they are not remote at all and perhaps after all the people there are just as well not being particularly conscious of them. In Mr and Mrs Egan's pleasant homely guesthouse, St. Ann's in Galway Woodquay, I renewed the acquaintance of Michael (Jack) Collins and his wife Nellie on their annual holiday to Ireland and Britain. Natives of the Turloughmore area Jack and Neillie now live in New York and Jack is the author of a published account of one of his tours of Ireland, 'Where England Made Slaves' a copy of which he was kind enough to present to me. Over a jar in the Central Bar up the way, Jack, myself and Tom Connell from Menlo discussed a great many things and, time being the scarce commodity that it is, left as many more untouched, alas. A man of unyielding Republican principles Jack Collins has yet a considerable affection for England where he worked for many years before emigrating to the States; he was to have called on me here in Northampton in the Autumn but through one of those unfortunate incidents, all to common these days for tourists, the theft of some baggage, his plans went a bit awry and it was lucky that unexpectedly, we met up in Galway.

Back in Dun Laoghaire a little worse for wear I looked out across the light-dappled harbour and tried to reckon up how many times I have made this short sea crossing; at a fair average of three times a year over 32 years it must be near enough a hundred. And with the help of the Man Above there will be a few more runs yet to go.

ID 11-MCMLXXX111

Chapter Six

POET, PROFESSOR AND GENIUS

They say that everybody has a book in him, or her, but not every body sets out to prove it. I never doubted for a moment that I had a book - a masterpiece, in fact, and on New Years Day, Nineteen Forty Three, I sat down to write it. The choice of date was deliberate, an auspicious occasion, I felt, to begin so momentous a task. We lived in Kilkenny then, in the upper half of a tall old house that had a cobbled courtyard at the back; the courtyard, I fancied, had once echoed the clomp of Cromwell's horses and the menacing jingle of spurs - you couldn't ignore history in Kilkenny, it was that kind of place. I had just left school and already I was making the painful discovery that employers weren't exactly falling over themselves in the eagerness to offer me work; I had exhausted nearly all the possibilities and the prospects looked bleak. My book, I intended, should make me my own boss along with bringing me fame and fortune, and no publisher, I was confident, could fail to be impressed by the grandeur of the opening paragraph. It read: "Not far from the bank of a murmuring stream, on the edge of the brooding forest, a lone Blackfoot warrior sat by a smouldering fire, his noble features composed in sombre thought." My book - which I titled The Last Warrior with an ornate flourish - was not the first expression of literary effort on my part. I had already written a couple of short stories in Irish, both of them about starving Munster peasants staging a futile revolt that was put down by the English with predictable ferocity. But I no longer wanted to write about Ireland. Ireland was too familiar and workaday, it was the scope and colour of the great American West that fired my imagination. That alone, I felt was worthy of my pen. My pen, by the way was a green Conway Stewart, a lucky acquisition which on the dubious principle of finders-keepers, I had claimed as my own. All my writing was done on sheets of close-ruled quarto that sold at four pence a slim bundle in Woolworth's up in the High Street. Writing paper was in short supply in those wartime days and even at four pence a time it was only my mother's thrifty budgeting that assured the progress of my book. We knew all about austerity in our house along before Sir Stafford Cripps made the word fashionable.

My Magnum Opus as I proudly called it was penned in a style that derived in equal measure from Sir Walter Scott and J. Fennimore Cooper, full of long verbose descriptions of the Rocky Mountains, frequent little sermons and asides and exhortations to the gentle reader to pause and reflect on some sublime truth; all the characters with the exception of the lone Blackfoot warrior, had impeccable Anglo-Saxon names, and the book's underlying assumptions were pure Hollywood bunkum. Like most of my generation I was an avid picturegoer. I had hardly got started on my Magnum Opus when a job turned up, a job in the woollen mills at eleven shilling a week plus a monthly bonus of two pounds - this bonus being conditional on my good behaviour and the vagaries of a benevolently eccentric employer. You could never bank one hundred per cent on getting the monthly bonus though you generally did.

"Thanks be to God and his Blessed Mother!" my own mother said the day I rushed home with the news of the job. "The few shillings will be a great help and you'll have bags of time for writing later." Indeed I would: the job, I determined, must not be allowed to interfere with my real vocation; and so write I did, night after night, in a fever of creativity, filling both sides of the page with never a pause for correction or revision, or to cast a critical eye back over what I had written. Somerset Maughan, I read somewhere, believed that most writers made up what they wrote as they went along and this was certainly true in my case for I never knew at the start of a chapter how it was going to end and I roped in fresh characters with all the enthusiasm of an old-time pressgang. I never doubted the excellence of what I wrote and as time went on my burgeoning manuscript symbolised for me an escape from the life of dull toil that faced everyone else at the mill. I'd pack in my job as soon as the book was published and thereafter my life would be that of any successful author, sunbathing in the Bahamas or lunching with my publisher in some fashionable restaurant. In the meantime, though, reality was a little different - snipping knobs of sheep-dung from oily fleeces, emptying steaming vats of dyed wool or packing bales in the blend room where a great bellowing machine spewed out a fluffy, multicoloured blizzard. I didn't actually boast that I was writing a book but the word somehow got around and soon I was being accorded the respect that was due to what my fellow workers called a brainy chap. An old weaver with more goodwill than gumption went so far as to declare me a genius and I didn't feel obliged to contradict him. It wasn't all goodwill, to be sure; there was the odd begrudger who claimed that a bit of skill on the hurling field was worth all the books ever written and others who would rather throw the half-hundredweight a fair distance than have a shelf-full of books to their credit. Their philistinism didn't bother me, however; I could afford to ignore it, I was only biding my time. There was one chap, though, who really did get up my nose, a tall countryman by the name of Tim Shanahan who considered himself a bit of a poet. Tim Shanahan's poetry was in the traditional ballad mode and though I didn't think much of the many verses he insisted on reciting to me I forbore to make adverse comment. Would Longfellow or Wordsworth sneer at some simple country rhymer? But Tim Shanahan was a nuisance in other ways, too. The poor man had a fondness for drink and on our way home from work on Friday evenings he would seek to entice me into the pub where he invariably remained until he was thrown out at closing time several hours later. Tim's blandishments and entreaties I rebuffed with a proper disdain. I was under strict instructions not to open my pay packet until I got home and in any case I had more important things to do with my time - I had a literary career to pursue. And so I would abandon poor Tim to his weakness, pitying him smugly as I strode home with my wages intact. Strangely enough I never dwelt on the progress of my book during the day although my work in the mill didn't call for much concentration. Instead I indulged in my Hollywood day-dreams, picturing myself with glamorous women in lavish surroundings light years away from anything I had ever known. And my fantasy was encouraged, if anything, when I got to know Professor Brophy.

Professor Brophy cut an old-fashioned figure even then with his wispy white locks under a black homburg, gold-rimmed, half-moon glasses, his black clerical garb with trousers that stopped well short of his ankles, white starched shirt and a black floucy tie that you only saw in cowboy films in those days. Distinguished looking older men hold some appeal for attractive young women and Professor Brophy was often surrounded by classy-looking girls whose conversation I imagined to be full of literary allusions and casual references to cities like Paris and London. Girls whose intellectual horizons, I felt certain were immeasurably wider than those of the mill girls tending the spinning mules and the clamorous looms. I used to picture myself in the company of the Professor and his young ladies, sipping cafe au lait in some leafy French boulevard and discussing famous painters like Renoir and Lautrec. My knowledge of these artists I gleaned from the books in the arts section of the public library, and it was from these books too that I corrected my somewhat erroneous notions about the female anatomy. The Professor never failed to greet me when he had his girls in tow but he rarely detained me for long and thus I was denied entrée to their exclusive circle. I wasn't too greatly disturbed, however, for the Professor had expressed keen interest in my literary work and had promised to read the manuscript as soon as it was completed. He might even be able to suggest a likely publisher, the Professor said, and I knew it was only a matter of time before I was hob-nobbing with thc toffs on an equal footing. I wouldn't always be a mill worker in oily overalls! And so night after night I scribbled away like some Victorian penny-a-liner, adding to my already bulky manuscript and happily unaware that not even A.G.Cronin himself would have his work accepted if he wrote on both sides of the page. My mother took a loyal interest in the progress of my Magnum Opus although not to the extent of reading the manuscript. It would be more enjoyable in book form later on, she opined diplomatically.

I finished The Last Warrior in the Spring of Nineteen Forty Four and I placed the thick wedge of quarto in an old biscuit box with mixed feeling of regret and satisfaction. It was a Saturday afternoon, I remember, and after tea I set off for the Railway Hotel where Professor Brophy had rooms, my precious box under my arm. But the Professor was out and so I entrusted my book to a curious member of the staff with some misgivings, stressing that the Professor was particularly anxious it should be delivered to him safely, and that I'd call back for it again in a week's time. I returned home then to await the verdict with quiet optimism - it was a very long week.

Professor Brophy had company the next time I called at the hotel - two captivating girls - but I could see at once that he didn't want me to stay. My book was ready and waiting in its tin box, he had read it, yes, and his comments were inside. Almost before I realised what was happening I was out in the street again with my biscuit box, not too greatly disconcerted but a little miffed that I hadn't been introduced to the girls. They'd have appreciated meeting a writer, no doubt - but perhaps next time! I curbed my impatience until I crossed the bridge over the silent Nore and there I turned left toward the men's lavatories by the gates of the Canal Walk; then, with racing heart and trembling fingers I prized the lid off my tin box and read the Professor's comments. They were short if not sweet, a couple of terse paragraphs to do with spelling and grammar and the infelicity of the split infinitive - and nary a word at all about the book itself or to which publisher I should send it! I was flabbergasted, astounded, appalled! Had the doddering old fool troubled to read it at all, I asked myself in anguish, or did he think I was one of his bloody students writing an essay on "A Day at the Seaside"?

But he had read it alright, at least the first twenty pages because these were scored with wicked red marks, corrections every last one of them, and testy little marginal annotations. It was as if an art critic had concentrated on the frame of some beautiful painting to the exclusion of the picture itself. Heart-scalded and seething with indignation I put my manuscript back in its box and ignoring the pleasant 'Goodnight' of the tipsy countryman relieving himself gratefully against the lavatory wall, I crossed over to Rose Inn Street, blind to the world about me. There was very little traffic in Kilkenny in those days but if a Sherman Tank had rumbled over John's Bridge I'd have walked under it, so great was my state of shock. And, then, as if to add insult to injury, I ran into Tim Shanahan in Rose Inn Street. "Ah, 'tis yourself!" Tim greeted me with the easy camaraderie of the boozer. He was already three sheets to the wind. I don't think that poor Tim can have been aware of the look of cold loathing I gave him for he demanded the pleasure of my company there and then. "We'll adjourn to Pat Henderson's," he announced, generously dismissing my boorish protest that I hadn't a tosser. There was fresh sawdust in Henderson's, the sweet smell of porter and the homely tang of pipe tobacco; Tim Shanahan opted for the snug inside the door and ordered two large bottles of stout - squat green objects with long narrow necks from which the smoke curled like a liberated genie when the corks were drawn. A potent brew! "Good health!" Tim proposed and I grudgingly returned the salutation. The stout was prickly to the tongue and the creamy brown froth tickled my nostrils; I shivered at the first mouthful and set my glass down on the sawdust like Tim. "That's a master large bottle," Tim Shanahan declared. "The best in Kilkenny!" I made no comment but such is the resilience of youth that I had already begun to recover some of my confidence. I had misjudged Professor Brophy, mistaking him for a savant when he was only a pedant - an ould dominie as Boswell's father said contemptuously of Doctor Johnson, obsessed with his piddling little rules of grammar. Hump him, I though, and drained my glass like a man. "Good man yourself! We'll have another," Tim Shanahan urged, and this time I didn't demur. We had almost finished our second drink when Tim became curious about my tin box. "What have you there with you?" he asked; and with bruised pride I took out my fat wad of quarto. "That," I announced grandly, "is my masterpiece - my Magnum Opus!" "Indeed!" said Tim, marvelling at the bulk of the manuscript. But he made no effort to read it and he handed it back to me almost at once. "We're two of a kind," Tim said with smug chumminess, "a poet and a writer!" I was dumbstruck, outraged, bowled over by the calm effrontery of the man - how dare he make so presumptuous a comparison, putting his pathetic doggerel on a par with my work!

"Yes," Tim went on with a silly smirk on his face, "as a matter of fact I knocked out an ould poem the other day. Would you like to hear it?"

Choking I nodded, and that was all the encouragement he needed. He removed his cap in accordance with some odd notion of etiquette, closed his eyes and began.

"I recall as once I wandered through Kylefarney's sheltered ways,
the sinking sun o'er all the land was shedding its last rays,
I met a weary traveller near the church of Ballyfoyle,
and I halted in my ambling, to converse with him awhile.

Tim open his eyes then and looked at me expectantly but no word of praise passed my lips. "Well?" he prompted eagerly. "What do you think of it?"

It was time for diplomacy - for common good manners, even - but black bitter bile was rising within me like a cobra's venom and all I wanted was to bring the drunken braggart down to earth. "It's rubbish Tim," I told him with cold cruelty, "sheer unadulterated rubbish!" Tim leapt to his feet, face flushed at this unwarranted insult, and it was more by good luck than by judgment that I managed to dodge the angry swipe he made at me. The cramped little snug was no place to start a row and in a twinkling Pat Henderson had us out on the street, me and my masterpiece and the mortally offended poet. We parted, hurling invective over our shoulders, and a little later I staggered in home a true Bohemian. I consoled myself, as I dumped my precious book on the table.

The closest I ever came to having my book published was an offer from a company somewhere in England to bring it out between hard cover for a fee of eighty pounds, an unthinkable sum of money in those days. And so The Last Warrior lay in its box for a year or more when a younger brother with a speculative streak bought the manuscript and copyright for a half-crown. I spent the half-crown on three pints of Guinness, which, much and all as I had come to appreciate the work, was poor recompense for my long months of labour. The brother fared no better than me in his efforts to get the book published and after a time it disappeared mysteriously, along with the box that contained it. The brother has always maintains that I stole the book back from him but, so help me God, I didn't! But to this day I have a recurring nightmare that The Last Warrior has surfaced somewhere and will be published with my name on the cover.

ID VIII-MCMLXXXV

Chapter Seven

THE STORY OF MR. BARKER

RACISM isn't a word you heard very often thirty-odd years ago yet there was plenty of racism about. Whether we are getting any better or not is a thing you could argue about for a long time but I'd rather just tell the story of Mr. Barker as I know it.

I was working as a ward orderly in a hospital at the time - 1951 it was. Jobs like that were ten a penny then and they couldn't get enough people to fill them. The National Health Service scoured Ireland for talent and I got my job through an advertisement in the Irish Press. Two thirds of the workforce was Irish I'd say and there was a clear distinction between the nursing staff, which included orderlies like myself, however little we know about nursing, and the ground and domestic staff. We had separate sitting rooms and ate in separate dining rooms and fraternisation wasn't exactly encouraged. The place was like the Tower of Babel there were so many languages spoken, but there was never a black person among us, until Mr. Barker came along.

His name wasn't Barker at all, actually, but M'Baka, which is perhaps not too dissimilar. It was Olive the cleaning woman who first called him Mr. Barker - either unwilling or unable to get her tongue around the full sound of "Umm-bakka" (a very satisfying sound I though at the time!). Unlike any other arrival Mr. M'Baka's fame preceded him - we were warned in advance of his coming. Mr. Pius M'Baka was studying medicine at Trinity College Dublin and rather than return home to West Africa for the summer break he was coming to England to gain practical experience of hospital life and presumably to earn a few bob - £4.7.0d to be precise for a 44 hour week!

Mr M'Baka, we were told by the Assistant Matron who warned us of his coming, was a chief's son, a man of education and refinement, and we were on no account to pay any heed to his colour, less still to pass any ill-bred remarks. I suppose we must have advanced since then a bit because it would be unthinkable today for any Matron or Assistant Matron to issue such caveat. But these were frank times indeed and in his recently published book Dr. Noel Browne tells us that a noted surgeon in TCD, during Browne's time there as a student, declared openly that he would not lecture to any "Niggers, Jews or Catholics!" So perhaps - and considering that to the best of my knowledge there was only one other black resident in Northampton at the time - it wasn't too surprising that the nursing staff should be warned not to offend Mr. M'Baka by any untoward reaction.

We awaited Mr. M'Baka's arrival with some interest. But there was a problem of accommodation. The nursing staff slept in small cubicles, two beds to a cubicle, and though there were beds a plenty the question was where Mr. M'Baka should be put. That was Olive's, the cleaning lady's problem and she expressed some perplexity to me on the matter. "Dunno where I'm going to put Mr. Barker, Pat. I mean," she went on without batting an eyelid, "it ain't as if we can have him sharing with a white man, is it? "Tell you what, I'll move old Brendan out of his room in along with you", - there was a spare bed in my cubicle at the time - "and I can put Mr Barker in Brendan's room. But that solution didn't suit me at all however it might have suited Olive. Put Mr Barker in with me, I begged, he was heartily welcome, anyone only not Brendan O'Shaughnessey! Brendan was an antichrist, no point in mincing words; the greatest pest and plague that ever left Mary Horan's Land; a cantankerous, bad tempered, inebriate, bellicose bastard. I didn't want him within a mile of me, never mind sharing the same room. But poor Olive was appalled. "Oh no, Pat, can't do that! It wouldn't be right - not a black man!" I begged for the pleasure of Mr Barker's company in vain but at least I wasn't lumbered with Brendan. Olive found a solution, which to her way of thinking was a fair compromise. She separated two Ukrainians, putting one of them in with the bold Brendan and making room for Mr Barker with the other. The other was a little chap getting on in years who had a stub of a wet fag in his mouth all through his waking hours and spoke fluent if utterly incomprehensible English. I felt sorry for Pius M'Baka. Pius, when he came, was as unlike your stereotype Hollywood black man (which was all any of us had ever seen at the time) as Oscar Wilde was unlike one of Murphy's heavy diggers. You could see right off he was a chief's son - he had that kind of languid arrogance about him that can only come from an aristocratic background whether black or white. He arrived and we were all on our best behaviour before him. It was only yours truly, I regret to say, who made something of a gaffe, and that from the best of intentions. Out of the depths of my naivety and ignorance I struck up a conversation with Mr M'Baka at the dining room table and began asking him about life in Africa. Not, I blush to admit now, the kind of informed and intelligent questions which any young man of twenty four should be able to ask, but bloody silly questions about snakes and lions! A weary smile flickered across Mr M'Baka's face and he hastened to assure me that his acquaintance with reptiles and big cats was quite minimal. Then, somewhat disconcertingly, he went on: "I was under the same kind of misapprehensions about your country before I went there - I thought that the people spent all of their time hacking and cutting each other with knives and pitch forks." He smiled indulgently at such nonsense. "Of course I found otherwise when I went there!" Mr M'Baka certainly hadn't any hang-ups about colour and his quiet air of superiority was a little hard to stomach. "Come along," he said to me on his first night in Northampton, "you can show me the town." We sallied out together, the six-foot, patrician Pius M'Baka and myself and I knew without having to turn round that a dozen pairs of eyes watched us from behind the curtains of the nurses' quarters. I showed Mr M'Baka the town and he commented on it as we went about rather in the manner of those old-fashioned travelogues, listing the industries that sustained the place and the architectural features that adorned it. Eventually we got fed up of this so we adjourned to the Plumber's Arms. The Plumber's Arms was a pub where the Irish held sway for most of the time though their hegemony was threatened once a month when there was an invasion of Yanks - both black and white - from the US Airforce base at Upper Heyford in Oxfordshire. The Irish lads drank beer or a horrid mixture of beer and stout called Black & Tan and they never brought girls into the pub. The Yanks brought girls and bought shorts with wild abandon. On the whole the Taffy guv'nor preferred the Yanks but couldn't see much hope of excluding the Irish when the Yanks were in town. There were fairly frequent rows between the white Yanks and the Irish and it needs to be said the Hibernians were mainly the cause of it. I don't know what they had against the Americans - I think they just happened to despise them in that prejudiced and irrational way that some sections of the human race despise others. In passing let me say that I don't think the white Yanks despised the Irish labourers they sometimes clashed with - their contempt was reserved for their black compatriots and their fights were more often with them. Massive pairs of Yankee military policemen, one black one white, patrolled the streets and they were quick to jump on any disorder. But that's all by the way ... Pius M'Baka and myself went into the Plumber's and we had a few jars. It need hardly be said that the African attracted attention - lots of it, but to be fair it was of a benevolent if maybe on reflection, a somewhat condescending nature. All that our lads knew about black folk was that you gave pennies for them at school - a fact, which I believe, is sometimes thrown at black squaddies on duty in Belfast and other such remaining corners of the Empire. At any rate they gathered around Pius and asked him how the crack was and what would he drink. Pius accepted their homage - for I'm certain now that's how he thought of it - very graciously indeed, assured them that the crack was sound and drank all he was given. I don't know if Mr Barker was skint as they say or if, like royalty nearer home, he never carried round any money. But whatever the reason he certainly didn't put his hand in his pocket that night ... The beer flowed freely, and the songs thereafter - The Valley of Knockanure and Kevin Barry; those were the kind of songs the Irish sung in pubs in those days - and Pius enjoyed his night. We returned to the hospital legless. Mr M'Baka stayed with us for the rest of the summer, until it was time to go back to Dublin and Trinity College again. I would like to be able to end this little tale by saying that we forged a beautiful friendship and that I think of 'Mr Barker' with fond affection still. I'm afraid I can't. For Mr M'Baka was a pain in the derriere, a haughty, conceited, lazy big aristo. Make no mistake friend - colour isn't half as big a barrier as class!

ID 111-MCMLXXXV11

Chapter Eight

TALKING TO THE BBC

'Keep yer hat on, they're sackin' the old 'uns!' - that's what the old-timers used to say hereabouts, the men who came through the Twenties and Thirties when it wasn't a case of jacking your job in for the hell of it, but a case of being lucky to be able to hold on to a job at all. I knew an old brickie who often told how the gaffers would sometimes sack a good worker - just to put the fear of God in the rest! You heard a lot of that kind of talk when I started working on the building and civil engineering in 1952, I think it created something of a bond between Irishmen like myself and the indigenous workers, a class interest in common, most Irishmen you met here if they'd had employment at home were pretty scathing about their employers, especially if they worked for the farmers. A lot of ordinary English working chaps were more radical just after the war than they are today, there was a great sense of independence among them and a willingness to be dubious about some of their own institutions; for example you very rarely hear anyone criticising the British Royal Family today, not in my experience anyway. But when I worked among Englishmen on the railway or on building jobs back in the Fifties there was almost always moaning about the Royals and the cost of keeping them all ... as an Irishman it surprised and almost embarrassed me at times and I tended to keep my views to myself, it wasn't my place after all to criticise the institutions of the host country! I'd knock things like capitalism readily enough in the course of a conversation if we had one but I was always conscious of that peculiarly touchy relationship that existed between so many of the English and the Irish - hang-ups, I suppose you'd call them. For two groups of people sharing the same language I think there is sometimes a lack of understanding, an almost total incomprehension of each other's perceptions quite often. I remember before the last general election, the time when people were saying that Labour's defence policy, or lack of it, would be the cause of a Tory victory once more.

Well I was talking it over with the contractor who was employing me at the time, a very fair and proper man indeed; I made the point that I didn't believe for a moment that the Soviet Union had any designs on Britain, that I thought they had enough on their plate with Afghanistan, as indeed Britain herself had a hundred years ago, I told him, Britain has not yet been invaded, not since the Normans defeated poor Harold almost a thousand years ago if,

I said, Britain were ever to be invaded the people here would fight like the very devil, they'd never accept defeat. Well, the boss-man seemed quite touched at this and says he to me in all sincerity: 'That's right, Danny, we've never been invaded - and nor has Ireland! And', says he with great resolution, "If ever anyone tried to invade Ireland we'd be down on them like a ton of bricks!" That man had been dealing in the course of his work with Irishmen on and off for years but he was blissfully unaware that English dominion over Ireland has been the course of friction between the two countries for several hundred years ... I would say, though, that there is a degree of acquaintance between the two nations now that you hadn't at all back in the post-war era - there is of course the common pop-culture that the younger people of both countries share to a degree they didn't thirty or forty years ago. Television is surely the biggest single cause of that but the volume of Irish emigration to Britain must also have had the effect of making us better acquainted, mutually, though I would claim that the Irish have always understood the English better than vice versa - for obvious reasons.

Britain has for centuries loomed large in the Irish consciousness as the conqueror must always loom large in the mind of the conquered. I don't doubt that such terms will seem hurtful - gratuitously so, perhaps - to many Britons who do not see things like that at all, who perceive the Irish as a part of a family of four nations, British in all but name. But that is how we Irish perceive it and I think you'd have to be stretching things pretty far to do otherwise. The British consciousness, preoccupied as it was for centuries with the larger world scene, with interests abroad and with the understandable concern for its own security and territorial integrity - it, naturally enough, saw Ireland and the Irish as only a small, and often troublesome, part of a larger whole; we, on the other hand, were all but obsessed with our powerful neighbour, though of course the relationship between us was far more complex than many Republicans would care to recognise. That is history but there was a great awareness of it - too much some would say - on the Irish part. A regular part of an evening's entertainment in an Irish pub here in Britain might be the singing of a ballad that commemorated the execution of the Manchester Martyrs, The Smashing of the Van, some eighty or ninety years before; songs like The Valley of Knockanure and others like it, about either the War of Independence or the Irish civil war that followed it, these were a regular thing. Much of it of course was emotional pub patriotism, a surface thing... I remember when poor Sean South died in an ambush in the late 1950's, there was a song called Sean South of Garryowen and you'd see them waltzing to it and singing it enthusiastically in Irish dance halls in London and other places, but there was never any serious thought given - except, among the politically-minded, the very few - to what it was that Sean South and Fergal O'Hanlon and others like them were trying to do - initiate a war against Britain in the Six Counties of Northern Ireland. No one discussed the feasibility or otherwise of it and when in later years repressive legislation like the Prevention of Terrorism Act came to inhibit political discussion and the open expression of dissident views the majority of us acted as the majority of people would in any country by keeping our thoughts to ourselves and adopting what is described as the low profile.

But this sense of history was there and it served to maintain a certain gulf between immigrant Irish and native Briton. Up to a point, anyway: equally you had to acknowledge how tolerant and even well-disposed so many Britons were to the Irish influx, there was always that ambivalence on both sides, going back centuries. You only have to read the comments of observers like Carlisle the historian, or Henry Mayhew - people like that.

If the Irish were much maligned in the British press and particularly in the scurrilous Punch cartoons that consistently portrayed them as ape-like creatures, there were also honest and kindly-disposed people who made fair comment... I expect the simple fact of the matter is that it's a shrinking world and we all know a bit more about each other than we did thirty or forty years ago. Curiosity about Ireland has never been a strong British characteristic anyway, and even today, after almost twenty years of fairly intensive television exposure you will find people here in Britain who will ask you in all seriousness whether a town like Wexford is 'North' or 'South' or as I well know myself, if you tell them that you're going to Kilkenny they may ask you if that's where the trouble is! Not many people in Ireland could display that degree of vagueness about Britain.

English journalists writing about Ireland have long been intrigued or amused maybe by what they regard as the peculiarly Irish capacity for being anti-British in a general way and at the same time in going out of their way to be nice to the visiting Briton: 'Oh but there's nothing personal,' they quote their Irish sources as saying with what is generally thought of as typical Irish inconsistency. But this was precisely what I found about the men I worked with - the local people I mean - when I came here first. They constantly expressed what you might call xenophobia sentiments, they had denigratory nicknames for almost every nation in the world, the French were frogs, the Germans 'krauts' and black people were either 'wogs' or 'jungle bunnies'...

ex-soldiers who had been to India or the Arab countries always spoke scathingly about the natives in those countries - but for all that, on a personal everyday level they were tolerant and friendly enough towards any such outsiders who might happen to work with them.

I suppose we all remain partly blind about ourselves, nations rarely have the gift to see themselves as others see them and it is quite a revelation when that happens and you see yourself or your compatriots through the eyes of another group. By and large the Irish - certainly the rural Irish - did not share the prejudices of the British regarding the Blacks and Arabs and Frenchmen the Germans - not the kind of condescending prejudice that is a legacy of colonialism, I suppose, - but in practical terms they could be far more exclusive of such groups than ever the English could. I worked for an Irish firm, a very well-known contracting firm, in the early 1950's and I can tell you that most of the men in charge of the hiring and firing showed a marked preference, not just for their compatriots, but for men from their own part of the country, words like 'Frog' or 'Wog' might not have been part of their vocabulary but a Frenchman or an Indian would have got short shrift.

ID X11-MCMLXXXV111

Chapter Nine

NOT LONG FOR LAING

There was no mistaking the Berkshire burr on the ganger's accent. "Go right on up there, you'll see the office - have a word with old Golden Bollocks, if your face fits he'll start you!"

Not for the first time I pondered on the felicities of Public Works speech; the nickname referred to the Timekeeper whose job it was to take on new men. Years ago Timekeepers were held in general contempt by the older generation of labourer - the tramp navvy-type in particular - but sometimes towards the end of the 1950's (if you can put a date to these things at all!) a new breed of men seemed to come into the building and civil engineering industry and grunting gangermen who either started you with bad grace or ignored your request for work altogether were replaced by excessively polite office wallahs who gave you the impression, when you approached them about work, that you were one of the most important specimens of humanity they had ever had the good fortune to interview. Ron Wiggins was one such and he almost fell over himself in his eagerness to get me a chair. A job? Oh that was assured, nothing to worry about there at all, just let's get through the formalities. He even offered me a fag, so help me God! And that's another thing that has changed a lot on the building. Once upon a time, even when you were taken on, all regimental and kosher with your national insurance card and your P45 and your own true, honest-to-God identity, there were no formalities worth talking about to be gone through - no nonsense about next of kin or place of birth or owt else like that. In recent years I have been asked my mother's maiden name, again so help me, I suppose it's only a matter of time before they finger-print us! But now the range and variety of the questions you can expect to be asked, not to mention the case history of past jobs they expect you to reveal, makes the task of getting work just that bit more difficult. I'm talking about proper employment, of course, not about being hired by some cowboy operator who doesn't give a damn what your real name is - or who couldn't care less about your dear mater's maiden name - I once knew a Geordie who went under the name of Ahmet something-or-other! As long as those lads can dock the 33% for the Inland Rev they couldn't care if you called yourself Robinson Crusoe.

Ron Wiggins wasn't like that, in fact he was so incredibly nice a bloke that I wondered he hadn't sought a career in the diplomatic service; he chatted to me in a leisurely fashion for quite a time about a variety of topics totally unrelated to the business in hand and then he took my cards (this was when you still brought your comic-cuts with you on leaving a job, in the year of Our Lord 1975 to be precise). I could start tomorrow, transport laid on, travelling time, bonus, overtime - all the blessings of those halcyon days that seem like a figment of the imagination now. (Example: three years ago the pipelayer I was assisting in the new city of Milton Keynes kicked up hell one week when our bonus dropped below forty quid; now the same man counts himself lucky to get half that in bonus, working a lot harder). Transport next morning at 7am was a comfortable van with two or three of Laing's (the contractor's) regulars studiously ignoring the half a dozen or so new starters - is there anything as chilling as the building site, especially from the registered timeservers whose devotion to their employer so often assumes an almost mystic quality? God bless Daddy, and God bless Mammy, and God bless Sir Robert McAlpine and John Laing, Frank Taylor (and his buddy Woodrow) and the rest of them for they are honourable men. But I digress as usual!

Arrived on the job, no talk of work yet, nothing so indelicate; another little interview with Mr Ron W. is indicated, but this time, unless I misjudge the good man, Ron's manner is just that little bit more brusque, less friendly. But he is still looking after our interests and he issues the six of us with chits for the store. The job is in its infancy, only wooden or pre-fabbed buildings, offices, stores, canteen and such have been erected yet; so we make for the stores. Ah, what munificence, what open-handed generosity - nare a thing that you'd ask for, it seems, but you get, a far cry from the barbarous times when poor unfortunates strapped the long handled Irish shovel to the cross-bar of the Raleigh and cycled twenty miles to the Shannon Scheme or to a hundred other lesser jobs. I had admitted some small facility with the wooden float and trowel, I could bench manholes, finish concrete etc, I had shyly indicated, and so there I was with a wooden float, pointing trowel, snub nosed trowel, chipping hammer, lump hammer and bucket - and ne'er a bit of concrete poured at all yet! And for good measure I got a pick and a shovel, a pair of wellies, a yellow water-proof suit and hat - at which stage I begged the Dublin storeman not to burden me with any more. I had got the point, I told him: the store was an Aladdin's Cave in which you had but to ask to receive; I could always come back for anything else I might require, but for the moment I had all I could carry... And by the way, how do Dublin men always pick these storemen's jobs? I seem to have met more Dublin storemen in my time, over thirty years in that line of work, than any other variety; some of them, not too many, are friendly, and some of them are inclined to regard a rural Hibernian like myself as something that just came down from the trees; but very few of them display the reckless kind of generosity which your man did - that much I'll say for him even if he did insist upon calling me "Paddy". After we were kitted out there was an hour's respite or so in which we lounged round, getting to know each other, drinking cheap (but quite good) tea in the canteen and wondering what lay in store for us. I must confess at this stage as a far more worthy representative of the pick and the pen - the Donegal navvy-writer Patrick McGill - once did, that I had no idea what was to be constructed on the open Buckinghamshire stretch of country which had recently been savaged by the Big Cats and their Jaws-like scrapers; nor, to be truthful, did I care a great deal. It was a job and that was all that mattered, the money, according to Ron Wiggins, would be good to begin with and fantastic before very long so who gave a tinker's curse what we were building?

Not a bat until breakfast break at ten o'clock and then we were handed over to a ganger; to that same gentleman with the Berkshire burr and the rolling r's I had asked about a job the day before; I had thought him a jolly sort of individual then, thick-set, rural, dependable and quite smart in his yellow-backed donkey jacket, plastic helmet and collar and tie, but now, like Comrade Wiggins he seemed to have undergone a slight metamorphosis if I may indulge myself with the use of the word. In fact, not to put too fine a point on the thing, he was quite unfriendly - suggesting in less than courtly language that we might like to get off our rear ends and give him the pleasure of introducing us to a spot of old-fashioned work. In some trepidation, and with even a rebellious murmur here and there, we did as he wished and trooped down the dirt road, burdened with our accumulated treasures, oilskins bright yellow, manual excavation equipment, to wit, picks and shovels, labourers for the use of, and all the rest ... The Berkshire ganger's name was Rick; he told us so, adding that he would not be requiring the courtesy of a "Mr" - nor needless to say, would he be titling ourselves in such manner - but that his surname was Benson if anyone was interested.

And then he put us to work.

ID VII-MCMLXXXIII

Chapter Ten

RETURN TO DUBLIN

I gulped slightly when the booking clerk said 'Seventy one pounds, please!" - Rugby to Dublin return rail and Sealink, that is. Going midweek and returning ditto you could save thirteen quid, which isn't to be sneezed at, but we can't always regulate our journeys with a view to taking advantage of the cheaper rates. Oddly enough the booking clerk referred to my seventy-one pound ticket as a 'high-saver' - a misnomer if ever there was one! The Supabus service must be taking a lot of custom off British Rail and CIE these days but unless you live in one of the departure points - Liverpool, Birmingham or London to name three, there isn't all that much to be gained and anyway give me the comfort of the train, you can stretch your legs and relieve your bladder, if you'll pardon the expression. And on the Caer Gybi (Holyhead) run if you travel day-time as I did, the scenery is very well worth watching from Chester onwards. The Sealink vessel Columba has had a bit of a face-lift since privatisation those horrid sticky rexine seats have been stripped and covered in some kind of tweedy material which is a big advantage, the bar lounges renovated and other things, too, improved like the duty free shopping area. The help-yourself carver lunch for £4.50 would seem to be reasonable though I can't say first hand as I didn't sample their fare - eating out, especially in Ireland, has become such a rip-off now that I prefer to bring a bit of grub in a plastic bag, a rake of old sandwiches, a hunk of cold chicken, and sup a pint or two as I dip unobtrusively into my bag. 'Eating your own' in pubs or ship's bars is decidedly infra-dig these days though I can remember, and not long ago at all, when no publican would raise an eyebrow if you brought out your 'sarnies' in his premises. It is all a part of the steady brainwashing of working class people so that they adopt middle class ways and attitudes. Not but that a lot of our working class attitudes could do with a bit of changing but it is getting to the point now where nobody wants to cater for a working man in dusty overalls or muddy trousers.

Overcrowding is the most persistent complaint we hear of the Holyhead-Dublin run; week after week we see letters in the Irish Post about weary travellers sitting on the stairs of the ship, which a conveniently located notice tells us is verboten, because there is not enough seating accommodation; there was plenty of room on the way over to Ireland even though, or perhaps because, each passenger had to secure a kind of boarding ticket before he was issued with the one you pay for, but on the way back it was very overcrowded indeed. Genuine complaints about poor travelling conditions are to be welcomed and it would seem that the Ireland services are not as good as the Continental ones but it seems to me that some travellers enjoy having a gripe... in the bar of the Saint Columba, a hefty, middle-aged Laoisman returning from a holiday in England was comparing the Sealink boat unfavourably with the B & I one he had gone over on a week previously; we were in a long queue, necessarily so, and the busy staff was doing its best I thought - but your man kept on and on, everything was better B & I, the bar staff more friendly, the fittings more luxurious and so on and so forth. I got a little tired of it all and, since most of his tirade was directed at my earhole I remarked mildly enough that it was a helluva sight better than the old Princess Maude (or is it Maud? - I can never remember!). The Laoisman however wasn't in the least consoled by that reflection, in fact he was rather incensed.

'Well isn't that it, now! Anything at all is good enough for Paddy! Put up with any bleddy thing some of ye would". It reminded me briefly of the night when four of us, myself and three Errismen, were making our way home through the then sleepy little town of Diss in Norfolk; we had more than a drop in and one of the lads in a playful mood stooped down to pick up a dish of water that had been left on a door step for a cat; the dish had the cat's name pained on it - Tommykins - and me man took a great exception to this. "Isn't that it, now?" he said (like the Laoisman on the Columba) "A drink left out for the cat - they think more of cats and dogs in this country than they do of Paddy!" With which, as the scribes used to say, he threw the dish of water as far as he could and, fearing the consequences, we took to our heels.

All is gloom and doom in Ireland now. The country is banjaxed, no hope at all, edging up for a quarter of a million registered unemployed and emigration reckoned to be as bad as it was in the worst days of fifties. I spoke to people who might be said to know what they are talking about, people in the media and communication world who have to know how things are going and they were almost as one in their belief that there was no Thatcherian light at the end of the tunnel, or should I say no light at the end of the Thatcherian tunnel... Garret Fitzgerald and Fine Gael are a washout, Labour a sick joke, the new PeeDees a thankfully small gang of fascists, and though most folk would welcome Fianna Fail back there isn't a lot of hope that things can get appreciably better under Charlie H. Why has the left failed in Ireland so signally? You could debate that one till the proverbial cows come home and I'm not even going to try and answer it here. It does seem to me though that among the many causes for the failure of our economy, emigration and the general helplessness all around is a lack of the kind of idealism that we once had. Sinn Fein would appear to be the only party with much of that commodity left today - the Irish language has been abandoned to them by the other political parties - but in view of what I see as the prevailing realities I don't think Sinn Fein are the people to get the country right.

There would seem a dearth of common or garden, practical patriotism in the Republic now and many of the young it seems to me are as much at home in the mental climate of Britain or America as that of their homeland; rambling round Henry Street one morning I saw young folk everywhere buying the English tabloids, not the far superior Irish national dailies - they are cheaper (the tabloids) to be sure; why wouldn't they when unlike our Irish papers they are exempt from VAT! The young share a common culture (if you can call it that!) too with the young people here in Britain in a way that my generation did not. Oh yes I know, in the 1940's and '50's we were brainwashed by Hollywood - at least those of us who lived in towns and cities were to a considerable extent. The country boys and girls largely escaped the influence - but culturally we were not anything like so much akin to the young people of the sister island as the young are today. If, as appears to be the case, the youth of Ireland are retreating into a kind of new provincialism; what hope is there for the country as a whole?

But if one thing more than anything else that I say in the course of my brief visit to Mary Horan's Land (as the old-timers here called Ireland) summed up for me much of what was wrong with the place it was the sight of a great hulking - he was hulking - Garda Siochana leaning with one shoulder against the wall of the historic GPO, his shirt clearly visible through the sag in his tunic, his whole attitude unmistakably one of sour boredom and, barring I am maligning the poor man, thinly-veiled truculence.

If this was a sight so rare as to occasion surprised comment I wouldn't worry at all - but I have seen Gardai singly and in pairs lounging at that same spot before with that selfsame air that brought so much adverse comment on the old-time cornerboys who, whatever their faults, weren't being paid-out of the public purse to hold up the walls. I don't know what the sight of a slovenly Garda Siochana lounging against the walls of the GPO in the principal street of our capital city does to tourists or foreigners - but I know it scares the hell out of me!

ID X-MCMLXXXV1

Chapter Eleven

THE CRACK

I joined the lads at the gates of the church, the same place we met every Sunday night after Mass. Mike didn't bother with Mass anymore but Peadar and I did; we wouldn't feel right if we stayed away. Peadar was lighting up, I took a fag and we hung on for a few minutes until the crowd began to thin out, then we set off for the Market Square. The Sunday night programme never varied - a game of darts in the Bull, across the square then to the Wheatsheaf to see what the crack was and then on to the Earl of Derby in Marefair to hear Sweeney play. Sweeney was a master fiddler but lumpy as hell, he'd play you any tune under the sun but the tune you wanted when the awkward mood hit him. I never cared a lot for Sweeney, more than once it came to my lips to tell him what he could do with his fiddle.

"We'll hit the Derby later on," Peadar said as though we ever did anything else; then just as needlessly, he added: "Sween'll be playing." There was something biting me that night, some edginess I couldn't explain and Peadar's remark irritated me. There was hardly a meg out of me all the way to the Bull and that wasn't like me at all. The pint of bitter was bad in the Bull, you'd think 'twas on purpose, and the snooty little Clare barmaid took her time about serving us. "That's a bad pint," I said loud enough for her to hear but the two lads said nothing. Mike was over at the jukebox studying the song titles - no more than Jim Sweeney below in the Earl of Derby you couldn't bank on getting the tune of your choice on the old dome-shaped Wurlitzer in the Bull, the titles didn't correspond with their numbers half the time and Callaghan, the guv'nor couldn't be bothered to put them right.

"Can't you taste it?" I challenged Peadar and he sipped at his pint cautiously. "I don't know, I see no loss on it," Peadar said though he was loath to disagree with me.

"You don't find it flat?"

Peadar sipped again, he'd as soon have found fault with it if he could be he shook his head reluctantly. "The divil a bit, Ned". Mike put his tanner in the jukebox and came back to the counter; he hadn't touched his pint of bitter yet. "Sup that, will you, and see what you think," I told Mike. The three of us had spent a few weeks of the summer up in Yorkshire at the hay and some of the lingo had stuck. Mike sampled his pint, you'd think he was wine-tasting the way he delayed about swallowing the mouthful of beer. Piss-taking, that was Mike's form when he was in good humour. "Well?" I prompted, impatient, but Mike took his time over answering and when he did he shook his head.

"I see nothing wrong with it, maybe 'tis on yourself it is." "She wears red feathers and a hoola-hoola skirt" boomed out of the jukebox, Guy Mitchell was all the go then but Mike pulled a face in disgust. "Doonaree, I wanted, that bleddy yoke is banjaxed."

"It seems," I said, "some people will drink anything". But Mike didn't hear me; he was eyeing the dartboard, his set of arrows out of their plastic case, smoothing the flights. There were a couple of McAlpine's men on the board; the stocky bloke in the navy blue suit and the yellow shoes wanted a double to win. Guy Mitchell warbled on unheeded and when the stocky bloke scored Mike jerked his head.

"We'll challenge these two - who'll mark the board?" I took the chalk, I'd as like mark as play and I wasn't too keen to do either, the bad pint was niggling me still. Peadar and Mike won the toss and Mike threw the first dart, double top straight off, no bother; they were away then and the two McAlpine men never came near them. Peadar was nothing special with the darts but Mike was a natural, as good as any of those fat slobs you see on the telly these days. Three games they won on the trot and then Mike put his darts back in their case, if they were made of glass he couldn't have been any more careful with them. "We'll have another before we go across to the Sheaf." Mike got that round and Peadar watched, as I tasted the drink. "Is that any better, Ned?" he asked, anxious to put me in humour. "It'll do," I mumbled, still huffed, and Mike made a great show of smacking his lips.

"Ah sure, 'tis mighty, what are ye talkin' about?" Mike was never too fussy about the beer, the crack was the main thing with Mike but later on he'd turn on the hard stuff. He looked back at Callaghan in conversation with some geyser at the far end of the counter, a rep or a traveller of some sort by the look of him. "Wouldn't you think he'd fix that shaggin' jukebox? Doonaree I was looking for". "Arrah, what odds! Come on over to the Wheatsheaf till we see what the crack is," Peadar urged, draining his glass. There was no crack at all in the Wheatsheaf, the bar was nearly empty wherever the lads were at all that night, there was only an old long distance kiddie with nailed boots and a muffler sitting inside the door and two Kerrymen at the counter, whispering like conspirators. I looked round the drab little pub and it seemed to me I was seeing it properly for the first time; what was I doing here at all, I asked myself, or was there nothing better in life but the same stupid old crack, the darts in the Bull, the crowd in the Wheatsheaf and down to the

Derby to get sloshed listening to Sweeney. "Aw Christ, it's like a morgue in here," Mike groaned, "come on away down to the Earl." But the guv'nor had seen Peadar and we hadn't the heart to back out again without calling a drink. "We'll just have the one." he said and called for three pints. We drank them in silence and then we drifted down to Marefair. It was like any other Sunday night and at the same time it was somehow different, there was a gloom on me like a cloud, I'd just as soon have gone back to the digs and the dingy little room I shared with Brophy who was too mean to go out. People get a foretaste of things, I believe, intimations of change.

Mike was striding ahead of Peadar and me with a rolling kind of gait, shoulders hunched in the typical navvy gimp that so many of the lads affected. Mike could turn awkward easily enough unlike Peadar and being done out of the usual crack in the Wheatsheaf had soured him. As we came near the Earl of Derby Peadar tried to brighten things up, imitating a flute player, an imaginary flute at his lips and his fingers dancing - that was an old caper of ours, drunk or sober, the busiest time we ever were on the job Peadar would make a flute of his shovel and I'd let a yell out of me or 'throw a step on it!' at Mike's urging, battering a reel of a jig with the heels of my boots. Down in Boreham Wood the year before we nearly drove an old Cockney ganger mad with those antics, bleedin' headers, he called us, bleedin' Paddy comedians! But I let no yell out of me now and I threw no step on it as I would another night, I couldn't bring myself to, somehow, not for all the tea in China. Peadar stopped his miming, abashed as a child asked to sing and then ignored when it did, and we carried on towards the Earl of Derby with an air of constraint thickening about us like a fog.

The sound of piano playing was coming from the Derby - for wonder: in all the time we'd been using the pub the lid had never come off the piano on a Sunday night before, Alf kept the Sunday night for Irish music always. "Arrah, the friggin' piano," Peadar said, disappointment stopping him dead. "Sween isn't in tonight." But Sweeney was there all right, he was sitting on his own in the corner of the bar, his fiddle still in the case, looking put out. And thereís a new guv'nor behind the bar, a big, bald, fleshy man with a ring the size of a shilling on his finger and a dicky bow under his chin; he had one hand on the beer pump like a man that would be eager for custom but his eyes were cold and wary as he pulled our three pints. Alf always had a word for you, but this new bloke was quite cool. We brought our points over to where Sweeney sat and Mike touched the fiddle case with his foot, almost disdainfully it seemed; small things could rattle Mike sometimes.

“What’s wrong you’re not playing, Sween?” Mike demanded and Sweeney pulled a face that could mean anything. “Start playing, for Christ’s sake,” Mike told him and the fiddler glanced doubtfully towards the new guv’nor. “The quare fella mightn’t like it, he has the piano going in the saloon.”

“Arrah, hump the quare fella! You play every Sunday night, don’t you? If the frigger don’t like it we’ll go somewhere else, a man’ll get a drink anywhere!” Mike was heating up and Peadar backed him. “Too right, Sween! Give us a blast.”

The piano had stopped in the lounge and the bar was filling up with the lads who came every Sunday night to hear Sweeney play, all dolled up in their Burton suits and white shirts, the navvies’ Sunday best; if Sween was to play at all now was the time to begin. “Go on, get it out,” Mike urged, he’d just as soon the new guv’nor made an issue of it, you could see. Sweeney took his fiddle out of the case but he spent too long farting about with it, tightening the strings and pinging them, a real Paganini. Before he got started the piano was playing again - Amapola an old Latin American number I hadn’t heard in years, not since they made films like Down South America Way. It took my breath, the heart-breaking melody, and without knowing it I edged over to the door of the lounge, the saloon as Sweeney called it though it was more of an old fashioned pub parlour with wooden seating and a scrubbed board floor. There were only a few in the lounge, old folks, all locals - it was always like that in the pubs round the centre of Norwold, the Irish lads in the public bar and the locals in the lounge, no friction at all just a kind of voluntary segregation. I listened in the doorway as the pianist’s thin fingers danced over the keys and the sweet melancholy of the air took me back a dozen years or more, Betty Grable and Don Ameche and all the wonderful bright fantasy of Hollywood. As a townie I was brought up on all that, Mike and Peadar wouldn’t have had a clue about it, I don’t suppose they’d have been to the pictures ten times in their lives. But then a poke in the ribs brought me back; it was Peadar, grinning happily.

“Sween is playing, Ned! The Mason’s Apron.”

I turned back to the bar, hiding my annoyance, and somebody closed the door to the lounge, shutting out the piano. Sweeney was on top form, I never heard him better, and he went from the Mason’s Apron to Roaring Mary with a braggart’s flourish. One of the boys let a yell out, a long undulating wolf howl, wow-wow- wow-wooooooo! with all the power of his lungs. It was the usual response to the music but I guessed that the new guv’nor wouldn’t like it and I wasn’t far out, his face was tight with disapproval and he had one eyebrow raised like an actor. Alf had never minded the yelling; he knew it was the lads' way of letting off steam, no harm at all in it. "Throw that off, Ned," Peadar told me, his own pint on his head. That was Peadar's style; the music made him more tipsy than the booze, and the minute Sweeney began playing he glowed like a bulb. I drank off my pint and Peadar brought three pints and three whiskeys down from the counter and it was the hard stuff for the rest of the session with the odd pint in between for the thirst. Mike never needed his arm twisted to turn on the whiskey though God knows he hadn't much more of a head for it than Peadar and myself. But even the whiskey couldn't banish the queer mood that was on me that night, nor Sweeney's playing which any other night would have me wahoo-ing with the best of them.

"Me life on you, Sween!" Mike bellowed at the top of his voice and the guv'nor glanced sharply in our direction. It wouldn't be long before he called a halt to the crack. We'd have been on the third or fourth short, I'd say, when the door to the lounge opened again; Sween was taking a breather and the piano music flowed in; Sibone, the tune caught me like a remembered fragrance and I pushed through the crowd into the lounge, closing the door behind me. Sibone, it's the tune that they croon down Havana way .. it brought me back like magic, the sweet nostalgia of it held me in a way that Sweeney's reels and jigs never could, I felt a tumult of pure happiness as the little middle-aged pianist in his shiny suit and National Health spectacles drew magic from the keys. It may have been partly due to the drink but I was carried away like a man in a dream, it seemed to me that the music had opened up forgotten vistas, as if it promised some sort of glamour and wonder in life. The door was pushing at my back and I stood clear to let in whoever was there; it was Peadar and there was a look on his face I had never seen before.

"I was searching for you, Ned," he told me, the anger making him breathless. "When I missed you and there was no sign of you coming back I thought you might be in trouble abroad in the gents, someone picking on you or something" - "I'm okay," I told him shortly. "I'm only listening to the music."

"You're listening to this?" If I had told him to push off Peadar wouldn't have been more offended. "You'd sooner listen to this racket than stop with your mates? Is that the kind of bloke you are, Ned - a feckin' turncoat?" How could I have made him see that I was carried away by the music, music that was as foreign to Peadar as the chanting of a Sioux beyond in Dakota? He wouldn't have believed me, I doubt if they ever heard Sibone in Mularanny. But I could have said something for the sake of our friendship, Peadar had been a good mate to me always, it was Peadar who brought me out on my first navvy-job when I was stuck in a stuffy little warehouse in London. I owed Peadar a lot but I said nothing, the contrariness had a grip on me now and incensed at my coolness Peadar grabbed me by the throat. "You're only a friggin' turncoat, Ned! I wouldn't think twice of planking you!". I didn't resist him at all, just shrugged as if to say carry on and just then I'd be as well pleased if he did, if Peadar struck me we'd be quits, he'd be as much in the wrong as I was. It was like something out of a dream, the pianist playing away as if nothing was happening while my mate stood there with his fist clenched, ready to strike. But he didn't strike me after all, a look of baffled hurt came into his eyes and he turned away from me abruptly.

"Stay with them so, Ned, if that's what you want," he said and went back to the public bar. There was another old favourite of mine playing now, Green Eyes, the song that Monty Ray was making famous when I was still at school at home in Carlow; but the spell was broken and I followed Peadar into the bar. The new guv'nor was calling last orders and I got three whiskeys before he draped the towel over the pumps, we'd have ten minutes to drink up and get out, they were very strict like that in those days. The bar was chock-a-block now but I managed to squeeze through with the three drinks without spilling them. "Well, fair play to you, Ned!" Mike said when I gave him his drink - if he knew about the few words in the lounge he didn't let on and Peadar took his whiskey with a shy nod. I had a sense of having lost something, of having gone too far like a kid with the tantrums. And then Sweeney struck up the Soldier's Song and we were all standing stiffly to attention, the normal conclusion to the Sunday night crack in the Earl of Derby. But something made me glance across at the new guv'nor; his face was white with anger and he was gripping one of the pumps as if he wanted to wrench it from the counter to use as a weapon. The moment the last note of the Soldier's Song was played he pushed through the crowd to stand, quivering, before Sweeney. "Take that thing out of here!" he told Sween, "and don't bring it back!" He drew himself up and then looked round on us all, he had been a military man I could see, an officer or a sergeant major at the least, it leaves its stamp on them long after they leave the army. "And you lot - if you intend coming in here again you'll learn to conduct yourselves! I'll have none of your bog-yelling here, it's not a shebeen you have back in Ireland!". I looked at Mike but it was Peadar who struck - one savage haymaker to the butt of the jaw, the sound of it like a gunshot - and the new guv'nor dropped like a sack. "Come on, Peadar," Mike said, suddenly sober, "the Johnnies will be here in a minute!" We walked home in silence and when we got to the gates of the church we didn't light up for a last smoke and a chat as we always did before parting. "Sod it, I think I'll pull out of this town altogether, there's nothing in it for a man" Peadar said as were passing the church. "Well, the divil a much," Mike agreed gloomily. We said goodnight then and I was sure they'd turn up for work in the morning but in fact I never saw either of them again. Peadar was killed on a big hydroelectric job in Scotland a few years later and Mike is now down and out and hanging round Hammersmith. A Mayoman told me that he hardly recognised him one day last year when Mike tapped him for the price of a drink.

ID 1X-MCMLXXXV111

Chapter Twelve

KIT'S STORY

Some break in the rhythm of track awoke me. We were almost there, I recognised a landmark or two, the Ovaltine egg-farm and the neon-lit Heinz 57 sign; it must be the dreariest stretch of ground in the world, the last leg of the long pull from Holyhead in the grey light of a January morning. There were only three of us left in the carriage, myself and an old Kerryman who had snored all the way from Crewe and Kit, stretched out on the opposite seat, shoes kicked off and the collar of her herring-bone New Look about her ears. Kit stirred as if she felt me watching her and opened one eye, ruefully it seemed to me in the poor light of the carriage. Then she burrowed again into her high collar like some small creature retreating from danger. It was Kit's first time away from home and not from choice, either. The evening before on the platform in Kingsbridge three Graiguenamanagh girls began to blubber when the "Rose of Mooncoin" came over the loudspeaker and from the look Kit gave them you could tell she didn't share their nostalgia. The music was part of the "Tostal" festivities but something less evocative might have suited the emigrants bound for Dun Laoghaire and the boat. The Graigue girls had boarded our train at Thomastown and we met them later on the boat, three wide-eyed youngsters trying to hide their homesickness and eager to chat with us and share their biscuits and sweets; they kept up a brave patter interrupted by the occasional wistful sigh but the familiar old song was too much for them and the tears came as they stood with their new suitcases on the draughty platform. Kit clicked her teeth and looked away in disgust; they had little to worry them, she'd have thought!

I had to rouse Kit at Euston, the old Kerryman was already awake, yawning widely and gazing speculatively at his callused palms in the way labouring men do, his battered suitcase in readiness on the seat beside him. All along the corridor doors were flung open in needless haste, travellers struggled with baggage and the meaningless crackle of the tannoy increased the confusion; you could taste the sooty steam from the engine up ahead, acrid as a leaking battery, and a string of trolleys clanked along the platform parting the crowd that surged towards the grimy columns where the black London taxis were lined up like a funeral cortege. When we were through the barrier I beckoned Kit and we went out the side entrance to Eversholt Street for a bite of breakfast at the Greek's. It was half an hour or so out to Norwold, Kit's destination.

“You could have left the cases in the left-luggage,” Kit grumbled, but it wasn’t worth it, I thought; the fortnight at home had left me short and every penny counted until I was earning again. “No bother,” I told Kit, shoving the heavier of the two cases under the table in the Greek’s where the smell of frying bacon filled the warm air and the windows were a steamy blue. The cafe was near-full, porters across from the station, building workers in muddy garb, a nightbird or two loath to go home. A sloe-eyed girl with full breasts moved briskly about, depositing plates of egg and bacon or beans on toast; Kit glanced about with distaste but she’d soon lose her convent-girl notions, there was too much false grandeur in Ireland. “Margarine,” Kit grimaced when the breakfasts arrived but she ate the bacon and tinned tomatoes; morning sickness wasn’t a problem yet, it seemed, but she looked a bit wan. We had left Waterford round three the day before and it had been a rough crossing. I felt strangely at ease in the cafe, comfortably anonymous and glad of the brief postponement of what lay ahead; I lit a cigarette, forgetting to ask Kit if she minded, and thought of the other times I’d come back off holiday with only myself to worry about. In a little over an hour I should be on my way back from Norwold, relieved of the burden. I eyed Kit covertly as she drew designs on the grubby check table-cloth, head bent, her thoughts her own; she was handsome rather than pretty, I thought, the kind that would improve with age, good clear skin and a wealth of dark brown hair. It was a pity the way things had turned out, Kit could have married well in time, but it was pointless lamenting it now. I hadn’t asked Kit any questions, I’d been too long left home to start acting the big brother; when I tackled Mam about it on her own she had shaken her head agitatedly and begged me to leave it so, what was done was done and we had to make the best of it.

“Mam will be up now”, Kit said without looking up. That was as close as she had come to admitting her loneliness, she hadn’t looked back at Waterford, even, and when the Graignuenamanagh girls got on you could see them looking at her with a kind of envy, her smart coat and shoes, her town-bred assurance. Things were in hand before I went home for Christmas, Sister Martina had everything arranged, Kit would go over to the Good Shepherd in Norwold until the baby was born, no one need be any wiser and the child would be found a good Catholic home. Kit would have no hard work in the Good Shepherd, Sister Martina promised Mam, nothing more than the office work she was used to. Mam had wept with relief but the thing would leave its mark on her.

"You'll come down and visit me soon, won't you, Tom?" Kit asked without raising her head.

"Don't you know I will? Coventry is only a couple of hours on the train." Kit looked up and sighed. "If it was anywhere else I was going but to the nuns!"

The Greek girl leaned across the table to take away a greasy plate and I waited until she had gone before reassuring Kit. "There's no loss on the nuns, Kit, you'll be all right with them." Kit gave me a wry look and I said no more. In the past year or so she had grown from an angular teenager into a young woman, it seemed no length at all since she was playing hopscotch on the pavement outside the house and sticking pictures of Eddie Fisher in a scrapbook. I thought of what she had done to her life and wondered how she'd feel a year from now.

"I'm sorry we ever though of them," Kit said without raising her head. "I'd sooner be going to Aunt Sarah in Romford."

She'd rue the day, faith... Sarah was a craw-thumping old killjoy and Kit wouldn't be long under roof before she had her transgression thrown in her face; colder charity than Sarah's would be cold indeed, the poor excuse for a man she had married hadn't the life of a dog with her.

"You're better off where you're going, Kit - Sarah is a right old bitch, didn't I stay with her when I came over here first? Wanting to know if you'd been to confession, an air of misery in the bleddy house. It's a wonder to God that poor eejit she's married to didn't take a powder years ago." I stubbed my cigarette on the saucer. "Will you have another cup of tea?" You didn't get a pot of tea with your meal in the Greeks, it wasn't that kind of place, you paid for it by the cup. But Kit shook her head and though I could have done with a second cup myself I hadn't the heart to call for it when Kit wasn't having one. And suddenly there was nothing to keep us there in the Greek's any longer. "Tis as good for us to be off, so? I prompted and Kit nodded. She was withdrawn on the train out to Norwold, staring dully at the sooty pebble dashed semi's with their pathetic little strips of lawn, the pinched respectability of the London suburbs. The train was made up of single compartments with no corridor and we were within a couple of stops of Norwold before we were on our own. That was when Kit turned to me, her eyes bright with a foolish hope.

"Tomsy?"

Tomsy... it was years sine Kit had called me that, not since her schooldays in the Convent of Mercy, it was always Tomsy when she wanted something, the price of a record or a few bob towards a dress, maybe - that was while I still had a job at home, before I went to England.

"What is it Kit?"

"Couldn't I go to Coventry with you instead of the nuns?"

I stared at her flabbergasted and she grasped like a drowning man at straw. "I wouldn't be a drag on you, Tomsy - honest, I could get a job, I could work for a good few months yet! Sure, couldn't we rent a flat, I'd do the cooking and everything, you'd have a nice meal to come home to after work, not the kind of stuff you get in the lodgings..." she broke off and looked at me in desperation. "I don't want to go to the nuns, Tom."

I felt like a man in a dream, the grind and rattle of the train seemed to be filling the small compartment like some invisible balloon about to burst, and like one in a dream I had lost the power of speech. And Kit, misunderstanding my silence, plunged on.

"Look Tomsy, I know you're short - all the money you spent over Christmas, the presents and everything, sure you were very good to us all. But I have a good few pounds here with me, I had some of my own saved and Mam gave me more and I leaving." She opened her smart shoulder bag and took out her purse, snapping the catch open to reveal a tight roll of notes.

"Thirty pounds, Tomsy, sure 'twill see us through a fortnight easily, rent in advance and all, what do you say, Tomsy?" The look on her face would pierce a stone but my voice was like a rasp when I answered her.

"Oh for Christ's sake, girl, do you know what you're saying? Go looking for a place in Coventry, and the way you are, they turn out married women with kids there, don't mind a young girl! You don't know how lucky you are to be going to the nuns, every care and attention, trained nurses and all and not costing a penny and no one the wiser, either." If I had struck her across the face she couldn't have looked more hurt; her eyes filled and she looked out the window again at the sooty privets and sad little lawns, her purse forgotten on her lap. Oh Jesus, I thought, why was I lumbered with this?

We had to get a bus in Norwold, the Good Shepherd was a mile or more away and to make some sort of amends I asked Kit if she'd like a cup of tea before we caught the bus. But Kit just shook her head and we waited uncomfortably in the queue until the red double-decker came along; I jammed the two cases into the space beneath the stairs, ignoring the conductor's aggrieved expression, and we found a seat on top.

"I don't know what you wanted dragging that case of yours out here for, you could have left it in Euston," Kit said, but I was glad to hear her complain, it signalled a thaw.

"Ah sure, what odds," I answered, relieved. The Good Shepherd was out beyond the edge of the town, a redbrick Georgian manor house with the newer laundry buildings half-visible at the back. A gravel avenue ran up from the high wrought-iron gates, a hundred yards or more, and there were flowerbeds newly raked and trimmed on either side. The Church wasn't short of a bob or two over here either, by the look of things.

"You'll be killed lugging the cases," Kit said with concern as we climbed the wide stone steps to the front door. "Tom?"

"Yes, Kit?"

"Take a few pounds with you, Tom - I won't need the half of this here."

"No, Kit," I told her, "Thanks all the same, I'll be back working tomorrow, there'll be no loss on me. Hang on to your money, it's always handy to have a few quid by you."

"Same old Tom - independent!"

I put the bags down at the door and looked at Kit; she pulled up the high collar of her long New Look and pinched her cheeks to bring the colour.

"I must look a sketch."

"Ah, you're fine, Kit."

I looked up at the great oaken door with polished brass bellplate and lion's head knocker, and the Order's insignia on the wide fanlight above; it seemed to me I could smell the waxed floors within, the austere spotlessness that went with starched white wimples and the swishing of black habits, the smothering, all- pervading odour of disciplined piety, the enduring claims of a jealous Church. I had my finger on the bell when Kit laid a hand on my arm.

"You'll be down before long, won't you, Tomsy? - Promise!" I stared at her for a moment and then I shook my head.

"No I won't, Kit. Come on away - we'll get the twelve o'clock train to Coventry!"

ID 1-MCMLXXXV111

Chapter Thirteen

THE WORKS

I met Maxie in the Cafe Pasadena just opposite the Works. The Cafe Pasadena belies its rather grandiose name because it is just an ordinary little transport "cafe" with one of those jukeboxes blaring unmercifully loud at most times of the day. I had not seen Maxie since he moved out of Northampton: in the interval, I had heard, Maxie had had an operation and it was only now he was on the way to recovery. It was early March and the snow still lay about in dirty-grey residual patches but the sky was bright with the promise of warmer days. Maxie got up as I came in, grimaced at the jukebox and got me a cup of tea. In cafes nowadays the younger generation invariably drinks coffee but Max and myself belong to the tea-drinking set when we aren't sampling anything better and so over a drop of watery scald we compared notes. Both of us had decided to look for a job in the British Rail engineering works across the way, our appointments were more or less at the same time and so in the manner of building workers everywhere we spoke of the advantages of a regular, secure job with a good strong union to look after your interests and numerous little perks such as free travel and full pay when sick. If Maxie, for instance, had been working for the Railway instead of for a casual builder when he was taken ill he'd be sitting cozy now and in no mad rush to get back to work. Yes, I agreed, and wouldn't it have been better over the past few weeks drawing a regular steady wage than being turned home again some mornings when the snow was too deep for work?

In the British Rail office across the way a very persuasive personnel officer outlined all the good points of a job in the Works; he was one of those athletic-looking office types who seem to spend all their free time in games like rugby and cricket and who give the impression of being much fitter than many a manual worker. At all events he painted a very satisfying picture of life with British Rail Engineering and in no time at all we had out minds made up for us. A medical followed and inside of an hour we were told we could start next day if we wished. So next morning Maxie and I presented ourselves at the office and in a little while a foreman came along to take charge of us. We followed him down a long flight of wooden stairs and my heart sank as we entered the heat and clamour of a great confusing workshop where hundreds of men, it seemed, bent over all sorts of incomprehensible tasks, a bedlam of flying sparks, grating drills and loud thumping noises. All the security in the world wasn't going to compensate for this, I decided, and wondered how long I could stick it or how long before I could decently make some excuse and escape.

Maxie, who had been in engineering some years ago, before taking up building, did not seem so daunted as myself but in any event the foreman led us right through this section and out into a yard where the cool fresh air and the silence fell like a blessing on us. There were other workshops with blackened brickwork and the unmistakable stamp of the Industrial Revolution about them stretching in rows away to out right and left but we had been assigned to the sawmills, it transpired, and here the noise that greeted us was the scream and whine of powersaws. The foreman led us straight through the mill until we came to a kind of raised office where he gave us a little peptalk before handing us over to the chargehand called Lennie. Lennie was an individual of the most truly astonishing limitations, a villager whose whole mental horizon was bounded by the four walls of the sawmills and whatever went on in and around his own home. He never read a paper or displayed the slightest interest in anything that went on outside his own tiny corner of North Bucks and he seemed convinced that mere outsiders like myself and Maxie could never hope to grasp the complexities of the kind of tasks which were our lot. And so Lennie would stand over us as we stacked little blocks of polished redwood, interrupting us from time to time to show us exactly how he wanted it done and then shepherding us off to the next job as soon as that one was completed.

That was before the advent of the pay and efficiency scheme and there is no doubt at all that the place was over staffed and consequently any of the jobs had to be strung out to the utmost for fear that we'd give the impression of not having anything to do. And in slack moments we were to go around the mill with brush and barrow, picking up all the chips and shavings and wheeling them out to the disposal bin which was collected daily from the yard outside. This make up job made a pleasant change because you got out for a breath of fresh air and a respite from the noise of the machinery but there was a limit to the number of times you could trundle out a handful of shavings and before the first break that morning both of us felt we weren't going to be rapturously happy in our new job. "But there must be other jobs we could do," Maxie declared. "God almighty we're worthy of something better than this!" "Oh, you'll progress," Lennie informed us between mouthfuls of cheese sandwich. "See all those men on the machines, they all started with the brush and barrow just like you two. You gotta prove yourself first." He paused to look at us proudly. "I had to spend a few years as an ordinary labourer before I was made up."

Lennie, it turned out, had never worked anywhere else but in the sawmills right from the time he left school; a benevolent management saw to it that he was never allowed to operate any of the dangerous looking machinery but I suppose his devotion to duty had to be rewarded somehow and so he was put in charge of the likes of ourselves - a responsibility which he took very seriously indeed. "You'll see," he promised, "you'll come to like it after a while and then when there's a vacancy on one of the machines you'll have your chance."

Maxie just turned an eye on me and groaned, but deliverance, for him, was nearer than he could have ever hoped. There was a maintenance gang employed in the Works; brickies, carpenters, painters and labourers and it just so happened that they were short of a man at the time and so by a lucky chance Maxie had collared that opening before dinner-time leaving me alone with the charge hand and the other three or four labourers whose fondest wish, I soon learned, was to graduate to one of the machines. "But don't worry, I'll put a word in for you with the building gang and it may not be long before there's a place for you there too," Maxie promised as he scooted off happily on his transfer. Watching him go, Lennie just shook his head in bafflement. "Can't figure your mate out," he commented sadly. "He had a lovely little number here if only he knew it and with a bit of luck he'd get on a machine inside of a year." ID 1V-MCMLXXV

Maxie, however, had chosen the better part and I envied him mightily as I saw him scooting up and down the mile-long yard on the builders' dumper with all the familiar accoutrements of the trade - picks, shovels, brushes, jack-hammers and airlines - stacked high in front. The maintenance gang was about ten strong and there was plenty of variety, plus the fact that the rate of pay was a lot higher than in the sawmills.

"Don't worry, old son, I'll soon have you along with me, you'll see," Maxie assured me the first chance we got for a bit of a natter. "I've been singing your praises to old Bernie and he reckons he'll be able to squeeze you in. But that depends on whether the sawmill foreman will release you."

Bernie was the builders' foreman and I vowed that I'd make such a nuisance of myself in the sawmill that my own foreman would be only too glad to release me and so I embarked on a programme of learning as little, or to be more exact of appearing to learn as little, about the workings of that department as would be consistent with even the lowest IQ. Thus I steadily resisted all Lennie's efforts to make me see what a wonderful place his department was and how lucky I'd be to find myself some day operating a band-saw, a circular saw or any of the other varieties of saw, the names and nature of which escape me now. From time to time Lennie would interrupt my sweeping-up and barrowing-out activities to bring me along to watch some particularly intricate piece of cutting.

"Look at that!" Lennie would exclaim enthusiastically, "Look how he rounds it off and shaves it fine as a butterfly's wing, Makes you wonder, don't it?" It certainly made me wonder how any man could be content to spend a lifetime bent over these same machines, endlessly paring and shaving and cutting until he grew round shouldered and waxed-faced. For that oddly enough was the complexion of nearly everyone in the sawmill - a corpse-like, waxy colour that put you in mind of some of the exhibits in Madame Tussaud's in Baker Street. Their destiny was to eventually retire with clock or barometer having been nowhere to speak of and done nothing out of the ordinary.

But let me avoid any misunderstanding here: I have no wish to denigrate a life of honest simple toil and most of the men who worked in the sawmills were models of quiet, honest industry, the backbone of any stable society. Building workers, however, by the short term nature of their employment and the constant moving about which that sort of work entails, develop a certain contempt for those whose employment keeps them chained at bench or counter. In the construction industry there is the illusion - and really, perhaps, that's just all it is; an illusion - of being free, and those who are free, or imagine themselves to be so, tend to despise those who are bound. About the best example I can give of this is something that happened while I worked in the sawmills. An outside demolition gang had been brought in to knock down some tall buildings on either side of the main gate and this dinner-time, as we streamed out in our hundreds, one of the fellows wielding a sledge-hammer high on the wall looked down on us and quite spontaneously began to bleat in derision at us, "Baa-baa-baa!" For no doubt that is how he saw us; a scurrying flock of sheep with no individuality or character. Nowadays when factory pay is fast outstripping that of construction workers, the thing has gone into reverse and it is very common to hear building workers express envy of those who do the same thing day in and day out at the same stretch of workbench.

Money, of course, is what it is mainly about and if the pay is right almost any job can be socially acceptable. I have known farmers' sons from Ireland who wouldn't be seen using a shovel in their own home place muck-shifting for further orders on the streets of English towns and cities because the pay made it all worth their while to do so. But to get off the digression; Lennie was quite dismayed by my failure to take a proper interest in the working of the sawmill, to learn the various types of timber, or remember just what went where. My addiction to the brush and barrow bodied ill for my future advancement, according to Lennie, and he would often come along and put a halt to my needless sweeping. "Ain't no need to keep everlasting sweepin', Pat, you'll have the bleedin' floor like the Locarno Ballroom where they do that Come Dancing thing on telly. Why don't you go along with some of the other labourers and stack the Indian teak?" The whole point of the sweeping business so far as I was concerned was that the sooner you got a few handfuls of chips or shavings in the barrow the sooner you could escape outside to the tip where a welcome breath of fresh air could be had while you leaned on the handles of the barrow and looked about up and down the long yard, listening to the hum and drone that came from the other shops and possibly glimpsing Maxie and Co., cruising about with dumper and gear, all set to begin some new project. The air in the sawmills was at all times dry and stifling for me. It was heaven to escape outside if only for a few minutes. This did not go unnoticed by some of the machine operators, and one day one of them, a kindly old chap nearing retirement gave me a quiet word or two of advice. I think I should remark here that if construction workers tend to look down on those who spend all their working lives in a factory, factory workers, for their part, tend to be equally appalled at the haphazard way in which we make our living - moving from job to job and often out of work for fairish spells in between. "You could have a steady little number here for life, Pat, if you watched yourself. Old Frostie, the sawmill foreman, is the best in the world and he'll move you on to a machine just as soon as ever there's a vacancy. I bin at this old gal, on and off, nigh on forty years and never seen no short time or nothing. But if they get the notion you're content pushing that barrow about you'll get nowhere." His heart was in the right place but I had not the heart to tell him that sooner than settle happily down to a machine job I'd pack up the job altogether. So I just nodded agreement, and went on with barrow and brush as before. Two weeks later that same old boy retired. There was a collection to buy him a retirement present, a barometer it was, depressingly routine, and old Frostie the foreman, made a speech in which he extolled the virtues of the old man who had given such long and worthy service. The old chap then made a faltering attempt at a reply, accepted his barometer and handshake, stumbled away overcome, and we all went back to our jobs. I knew then with all the certainty of death that I'd never qualify for a retirement presentation in the Works. ID V-MCMLXXV

The frightening thing about a routine job in which one does the same thing day in and day out at more or less the same pace is that before long a sort of numbing boredom takes over, a state of semi-torpor which can only be described as half living. In this manner men can be reduced to near-zombies and it is only their home or their hobbies that saves them from such a fate. Anyone who has come in contact with crofter people who have to do a diversity of tasks as sea fishing, farming and so forth to eke out a living will, I think, readily admit that such people often have a completeness and breadth of vision which can be lacking in the workers who must perforce stick at boring, repetitive jobs. But since there is apparently noway, even if it were desirable, of turning the clock back to a simpler mode of life workers caught up in the monotony of factory life must compensate by other interests. Most of the men in the sawmills, for instance, were keen gardeners and when they discussed their allotments among themselves over a quick pull at a cigarette outside the doors of their department it was with a keenness and obvious enjoyment that was lacking in their own work.

Irishmen tend to be a little amused at their English fellow workers addiction to gardening and indeed it has been said by someone of note in the past that the Irish are farmers by necessity and politicians by nature. Whatever about that it is certain that the Irish do not display the same love of flowers or gardens as do the English and in the Works whenever on Irishman inquired of another how the old kidney beans were coming along you might be sure that it was by way of sly jest rather than a serious question. Another thing about the Works, of course, was that being situated as it was in a corner of rural Buckinghamshire most of the men there had their roots in the country and indeed a great many of them had been farmers labourers in their time. A thing, which intrigued me about some of these ex-farmers men was that they never seemed quite to lose that healthy outdoor complexion even though many sections of the Works were very unhealthy indeed. Personally, I had been in the sawmills only a few weeks, when, in spite of all my little clandestine trips out with the wheelbarrow, I developed an unhealthy paler - and if I stayed there long enough and got placed on a machine, the permanent stoop that characterised the old machine hands would be mine as well. Fortunately, however, deliverance was on the way and Maxie came to me one morning in some excitement to inform me that there was a vacancy now in the building maintenance gang and that he had put a good word in for me with Bert, their foreman. All I had to do now was make a formal application and hope that my own gaffer would be willing to release me.

I wasted no time in making the application and the foreman of the sawmills made no objection; to be honest I think he had me weighed up as an unwilling member of the team and was only too ready to let me go. And so the following Monday I reported to Bert in the builder's shed and I knew from the start that this line of work would be a lot more to my liking. The rate of pay, too, was better and there were Saturdays as well which meant that I was going to be nine or ten pounds a week better off - a not inconsiderable increase in the old weekly income. Saturday was when a number of tasks, which couldn't be got through in the weekdays were tackled and one of these jobs, which we took more or less in rotation, was mucking out the bogey-wash in the lifting shed. The bogy-wash was a kind of pit such as mechanics use for getting underneath the vehicles they are about to repair. In this case the bogy's, after the carriages had been lifted from them, were stood in position in the "wash" and then high pressure jets of water turned on. The water jets made a good job of cleaning the accumulation of grime and filth off the bogy's but at the end of the week a thick deposit of dirt lay in the pit and had to be mucked out with shovels, scoops and buckets. Whatever of rags could be found were donned for this particular job and a dumper hauled the stuff away. You could stand on top and use the long handled scoop or ladle for a time but in the end it was better to squeeze into the pit and shovel the dirt into a bucket and pass it up to the man above who would then cart it out of the enclosed 'wash' and tip it in the dumper. Two o'clock was quitting time on Saturday but no matter how hard you went it seemed that cleaning out the bogy-wash took up most of the day. On a few occasions when we managed to get it done a bit early, old Bert found us something else to keep us busy until it was time to clock out, so there wasn't a lot of incentive, really, to go all out and get the thing done.

It was a pleasant change to be working along with Max again but I was more often partnering an old bricklayer, an Oxfordman of particularly cantankerous nature. Old-time tradesmen were notoriously hard to please. You could be at your wits' end striving to do things, as they wanted them done and never succeed. This one was no exception. I suppose I had better call him Ernie in case a copy of the Irish Democrat falls into his hands. But to be fair perhaps I would say that his temperament was more mercurial than cantankerous. For Ernie could be very pleasant on occasions; when things were going well with him he would become quite cheerful and even crack a few rather wilted jokes. Yet again he would break into an odd burst of song, hymns mostly, as he bedded the bricks in the soft compo and wielded his trowel with a dexterity that never ceased to amaze me.

'Men Scorn Thy Sacred Name,' was a first line of one of his favourite hymns but he had a very wide selection off by heart; indeed I don't think there can have been many lines in the Westminster Hymnal unknown to him. Ernie previously had a series of mates or labourers but most of the men found him so hard to get along with that a new arrival like myself was bound to be stuck for the job. After the heat and the noise of the sawmills, however, it was not all that hard to put up with Ernie, even at his worst he was a man of intelligence and perception but his politics could be described as a little right of centre. The troubles in Northern Ireland were just getting into their long and tortured progression at the time and I soon found myself in heated discussions with Ernie. Like the majority of the English working class he was horrified at the pictures, which were then beginning to appear on his television screen. Pictures like that never to be forgotten scene of a senior R.U.C. officer pursuing and battening a fleeing marcher, but his faith in the fairness and justice of Westminster remained firm. Alas, the events of the past few years have shown us all how wrong people like my bricklayer friend could be. ID V1- MCMLXXV

We are so accustomed to hearing the ordinary worker lambasted in the popular Press for not pulling his weight or even doing a middling day's work that one begins to despair of ever getting the other side of the picture. The pay in the Works was never what could be described as good by any modern standards and for lots of categories it was well below what used to be somewhat quaintly known as the poverty trap. Yet a great many of these workers who were in receipt of the smallest weekly wage were men and women who worked the hardest.

The smithy, as the blacksmiths shop was called, used to be a veritable inferno to work in, in the old days, but of course conditions have greatly improved; even so I always dreaded those infrequent occasions when there were maintenance jobs to be done there - the excessive heat and deafening noise, the air that was as thick and sulphurous as any roadside smithy years ago, not to mention the sparks that seemed to fly and explode dangerously all over the place. All this was enough to give me the shivers and I wondered how anyone could spend a year working there, let along a lifetime. For that is exactly how many of the old timers there spent their days, toiling away in the heat and dust of the smithy until the day they retired. I knew one old chap who had spent some forty years there but had never been up to the far end of the Works, a mere thousand yards or so! Journalists and business people who have the temerity to criticise the working class in sweeping general terms should come and see how many workers spend their lives and then they might pause before "slamming" the real producer of wealth.

The old brickie I was attending, like a lot more in the Works, seemed not to mind how rotten conditions were or how awkward the job that had to be done. I suppose, like a number of other building workers, I had seen such a glut of work in the 'fifties and 'sixties here in the Midlands that I had come to be choosy or as choosy, that is, as a workingman can ever afford to be. We often jacked up a job to go to another one that paid no more and possibly even less, merely because the mood to change had struck us, but most of the men in the Works, the old timers at any rate, seemed to be in mortal dread of making any move at all.

And so it was that these men, living in the midst of an area that was being rapidly developed and with good money to be picked up outside, elected to plug away at the safe, secure jobs they knew, grumbling about the money but still afraid to make the break. I mentioned this to the brickie one day, telling him that I knew for a fact that he would be sure to double his weekly earnings if he packed up and went to work outside on one of the new housing schemes. I told him I was sorely tempted to do so myself except that the free travel concessions were very handy for someone like myself who liked to go on a visit home to Ireland as often as possible. The bricklayer would have none of it.

"Yes, I know, I've heard all about that big money before but it never lasts, the job comes to an end, there's a strike or something and then where are you? No, you take it from me, lad, a bird in the hand is worth two in the bush." "Yes, and the divil you know is better that the divil you don't know," I matched with an Irish proverb.

The old brickie, like most of the men in the Works, had a rural background and one day I drew forth his disgust and contempt when I told him in some excitement about what I thought was an interesting discovery. We tackled little bits and pieces of jobs - concrete repairs, brickwork, excavations and so forth, all over the Works as occasion demanded and we were always in and out of different departments or 'shops' as they call them there. One day we would be working in the smithy, another day in the lifting shed, the day after in the machine shop and so forth. I began to notice that the men engaged in their work at the machines or benches would from time to time and for no apparent reason break out into a doleful chant which I could never understand but which sounded something like "OOO-ah, ooo-ahî!

It was really uncanny they way they would begin, seemingly in perfect unison, with no single voice leading the way; at one moment there would be just the drone or the roar of the machines, depending in which shop you were, and then without warning every one was giving tongue to that strange wordless dirge "OOO-ah, ooo-ah!" I mulled over this for a long time and then suddenly one day it dawned on me in a flash; all these men, practically, came from the small villages around about and many of them had worked on the land previously. They were steeped in the rural folklore of the district and no doubt this was some sort of half-forgotten worksong such as the old time peasant might have sung to relieve the tedium of a hard, long day in the fields. And so I communicated, in considerable excitement, what I regarded as my discovery to the old bricklayer. "It's probably the last living example of the survival of genuine folk music in this part of England!" I cried. The brickie, of course, looked at me as if I was a complete madman. It took him a moment to find words, and then when he did - he let rip.

"Well, Pat," he spluttered, "I always reckoned you were a bit of a queer 'un but if this don't beat all that ever was or ever will be under the Lord's heaven. Folklore? Work songs? Why, you blithering idiot, they're calling out 'Door - Door' - they want us to keep the f——g door closed and not to be perishing 'em with the effin draught!" He was too disgusted to speak to me for a good half a day after that and, suitably humbled, I went about the task of knocking up his compo and stacking the bricks within arm's length of him. I suppose you could give me a mark or two for imaginative ability but of course the old brickie was right and only a blithering idiot could have put the construction on the thing I did. ID V11-MCMLXXV

When I wasn't assisting Ernie I would sometimes find myself working with a much older man than myself, another labourer who was shortly due to retire. Tom Gooding was this man's name and he had a nature as sweet-tempered as the old brickie's could be foul. Whatever it was old Tom Gooding was sent to do he set about it with a will, never grumbling or complaining but getting struck in and working away at a steady pace that got him through a lot more in a day than many a man who fussed and rushed about. Old Tom had a singularly uneventful life, having held only three jobs in all, but, like many such people, it never occurred to him that his life might have seemed dull to others and he would go over the details of the three jobs he'd been in to anyone who cared to listen. He came from the little north Buckinghamshire town of Olney and as soon as he left school in the late twenties he got a job in one of the boot and shoe factories there.

In those days boot and shoe workers had to be very careful of their jobs and old Tom would tell how if you removed your apron a moment before the whistle went the foreman told you smartly to put it back on and not be so eager for off. The threat of the sack hung over you always and it was rare indeed to hear of anyone leaving of their own free will. Old Tom would shake his head, not altogether regretfully I must say, as he thought back over those times and then with a chuckle he'd tell of the day he made the dramatic decision to pack up his job in the boot and shoe trade and go out on the building.

"They thought I wuz mad, clean off me rocker, and they done their level best to advise me, but I'd 'ad enough, Pat." So Tom started work for a local building contractor and, as luck would have it, the nature of the work meant that he was exempted from army service when the war broke out so that he spent those years of turmoil and bloodshed fairly secure in his own county though not in his own home town. The work, a Ministry job, was some miles away but there was camp accommodation and Tom Gooding settled down there for the duration of the war, near enough. It was here that he made the acquaintance of Irish people for the first time and old Tom would regale me with tales of Herculean feats of labour performed by what he called some the of the old-time Paddies. Oddly enough - or perhaps so - what impressed Tom most about his Irish workmates in that camp was not their reputation for hard drink but their quiet and industrious disposition? With the ending of the war most of the men moved away as soon as the restrictions of free movement were lifted. It was then that Tom came to the Works where he was to remain to end his days as it happened.

I don't think I ever came across a man so completely at one with his life and surroundings as Tom Gooding. His pleasure in life was made up of the most basic and simple things - a walk with his grand child in the evenings, a meal of fish and chips fetched in on his way home from the pub. He would talk to me endlessly about his home and family. Englishmen are perhaps more truly domesticated than a lot of other races and certainly it would have been hard to find anyone more wrapped up in his home life than old Tom. He spoke of his wife with the utmost affection and if ever she had an ache or pain you might be sure that Tom would recount it in detail the next day. His was a very loyal and united family circle and all his sons and daughters with their own families would flock to Tom's house every Sunday and on the Monday old Tom would give you the ins and outs of their lives; how the kiddies were getting on at school and so forth. It seemed with him as if daily familiar things never grew stale and I am certain that he never longed for anything out of life other than that which was his lot; and when you consider what a mess this life of ours can be it would be hard to dispute that Tom was a rich man indeed for all that he probably never had more than a few pounds together from the day he commenced work. But, like many another man who worked hard and faithfully all his life, poor Tom was denied the reward of a long and happy retirement.

About a fortnight or so before he was due to be pensioned off he developed a slight pain and on being examined by the doctor agreed to undergo an operation, which, he was assured, would be nothing at all. Unfortunately the operation was to be the cause of his death - just another one of those cruel ironies that life is all too often made up off. Like a lot of the workers, Tom Gooding was genuinely puzzled by developments in Northern Ireland at the time and he would often ask me the whyís and wherefores of it all. And I would try, of course, to present as fair a picture as I could, not neglecting to attempt an explanation of the fears and prejudices of the Loyalist majority in the six counties, as well as the aspirations and grievances of the minority in that area, who of course were part of the majority in Ireland as a whole. But of course it was all so far beyond anything in old Tom's experience that I doubt if I ever really succeeded in making him grasp what it was all about. What was clear to me, however, from talking with Tom Gooding as well as with many another man in the Works, was the undeniable fund of goodwill that existed towards Ireland and the Irish.

This may have lessened with the course of events, human nature being what it is, but it was heartening at the time to know that there were no many Englishmen who cared and who would have been very happy to see a solution to the problem. Until recently I would say that most of the English were rather inclined to dismiss our pretensions to be different in a way that could be a little irritating at times. For instance, if you want it to be known that you come from an independent and culturally "foreign" country it is a bit irksome to hear someone tell you, "Nonsense, Pat, you're as British as we are! English, Irish, Scots or Welsh - what the odds, man; we're really all the one..."

What has become clear to me over the years, however, is that when the chips are down this oneness or unity matters more on a class basis than on one of nationality. For who could deny that the likes of myself is more akin to a man like Tom Gooding than, say, Tony O'Reilly, or any such Irishman today? ID V111-MCMLXXV

The train we caught in the morning to the Works was an early one. The two minutes past seven to be precise. But you could be certain that there were very few last-minute dashes to board her before she moved out because the majority of the men seemed to be addicted to early rising. It is easy to generalise, I know, but one cannot escape the impression that the English are better early risers than the Irish; certainly than the Irish at home in Ireland, for it is quite common to find shops unopened by nine or even ten o'clock in many a small Irish town. This was brought home very forcibly to me a few weeks back when I took a walk before breakfast one morning while on a couple of weeks' holiday in Kilkenny. I had thought to pick up the daily newspaper on my stroll but not a hope, there wasn't a shop open anywhere even though it was now about half past eight. Walking through one of those new and very attractive housing estates (council, I am happy to say), I did however pass two women, one of whom greeted the other something like this: "God save you, Mary girl, 'tis bright and early you're out!" I thought of myself catching Laing's van here in the English Midlands at seven o'clock every morning and grinned wryly.

The Works train was always packed and the occupants of each carriage even at that early hour were always full of the joys of life, chattering away about football or cricket but rarely about more serious matters; that or stuck in the "Sun", "Mirror" or "Express". It has never ceased to amaze me how thoroughly addicted to the Tory press the majority of the British working class seem to be, and I am not excluding the Irish workers in Britain - and indeed to some extent at home - from this. The "Sun" and "Mirror" make a show of being on the side of the worker but who can doubt that what they are chiefly interested in is the worker's daily pennies and not in securing a better deal for the working class? If, for example, the Labour Party in the present crisis were to set about implementing truly socialist policies to tackle the situation, what an outcry there would be from the popular tabloids, which only the continued support of the working masses keep afloat. The "Express", to be sure, is more overtly Tory but I often think that it is a deal more open and honest than either the "Sun" or the "Daily Mirror". Indeed, with regards to these last two it is not unreasonable to suggest that their main intent seems to be to prevent the workingman and woman from thinking seriously about anything. The amount of space devoted to trivial and frivolous matters alone confirms this, not to speak about the glorification of the rich and famous.

This is something, which I often attempted to counteract a little in my own way by offering some socialist newspaper to one of my workmates on the fifteen-minute train journey to the Works.

"Yes, Pat, but it's one-sided," was the invariable reaction, as though the popular press in Britain was anything other than one-sided and cleverly so at that! But of course if one is open to the same type of influence day in and day out, year after year, it is only to be expected that the old brainbox will be well and truly washed. It was always interesting to note how some of the middle-aged and older men in the Works reacted to outbreaks of violence either at home in Britain or across the Irish Sea. Almost without exception the violence in the six counties, which was now taking an ugly turn, was condemned and its possible causes ignored; the condemnation was always harsh and unqualified and of the "Hang-the-bloody-lot-of-'em" variety. One old boy in particular - a kind enough old man with very sterling qualities of honesty and industry - had his own solution to everything ranging from armed resistance to oppression, to common assault: "Hang 'em or shoot 'em, every sod that carries a gun and ain't in uniform." The fact of the uniform made violence acceptable to his way of thinking just as the placing of one bomb in a public-place nowadays is commonly regarded as being more reprehensible than the levelling of Dresden during the war. Another very common attitude to riots and violence whether in the United States or in Northern Ireland was "Yes, they MAY have grievances but that ain't the way to right them. That only makes things worse." Well, unfortunately, we all know how true this is and how little the Labour movement in Britain would have achieved if it had been content to wait hopefully for a better world for working people. Nothing has ever been gained without a struggle though to be sure a non-violent struggle on the lines of the Northern Ireland Civil Rights Association may often achieve as much if not more than armed conflict.

What I find almost as bad as much of the senseless violence we have become so used to is the complacency which seems to grip people everywhere today. It is not confined to Britain or to the working class in Britain - it is dangerously prevalent in the Irish Republic where prison conditions, for example, are far from satisfactory. Where prisoners are frequently ill-treated and you have a Minister for Justice who can blandly deny that prisoners have any rights at all. Such complacency can be detected in the letter pages of the daily Press in Ireland when arcane, academic or trivial matters can be argued over for weeks and yet there is scarcely a word when uniformed police and soldiers savagely mistreat someone in supposedly lawful custody. It is to be noted in the benignly smiling face of a senior clergyman watching the horrid spectacle of a live hare being torn between the jaws of greyhounds; It is my belief that our condonation of such senseless violence is very often as much a sickness as is the root and cause of the greater violence. But I digress from my story. ID 1X-MCMLXXV

One of the drawbacks about the building maintenance gang, I was soon to discover, was that two-thirds of the repair work had to be done indoors amid the noise and heat that was the lot of the engineering shop workers so that, except for the odd day out in the air or the frequent enough trips out to tip a dumper load of concrete rubble, you were almost as long under a roof as anyone else. Of course in the winter there were times when this was not a bad thing. Indeed when it rained and you knew building workers outside would be sent home with consequent loss of earnings or, worse still, work on, so getting thoroughly soaked. But even then there were lots of bright fresh days when you longed for a breath of clean air and when the brief excursion down to the tip or up to the stores for some piece of equipment became something to look forward to. Before long I began to think seriously of packing it in altogether and looking for something outside where things were beginning to pick up again after a seasonal slackness. However, just then a vacancy was announced in another department - the yard gang - and here I made history in the Works by being probably the first man ever to apply for a job with less pay.

The yard gang rating for some reason or other was the lowest in the entire Works and nobody at all wanted to be part of it. A new employee on being drafted into the yard gang invariably did his best to get a transfer as quickly as possible into some other section where the money was better and the work lighter. In spite of the "mechanical aids" as they were rather quaintly called, there was a great deal of heavy lifting from time to time in the yard. Barrels of oxide, for instance, had to be manoeuvred from the incoming wagons either by hand or with the aid of a sack barrow as they were called and you could give your back a very nasty wrench indeed while engaged in this particular job. Also there were frequent loads of pig-iron, and these had to be loaded by hand into wire stillages - a heavy enough task by any standards.

The transfer to the yard gang was not made too smoothly, for while they were only too willing to gain a new and totally unexpected recruit; my own foreman was not too happy to see me go. In the end he consented, and the following Monday I began in the yard gang, a job which I was to keep for two years - which in my case at least, was a considerable record. The yard work provided a fair share of variety with the added advantage that it was almost totally out of doors. There were four of us together as a rule, a tough old boy called Jerry who had been captured in the Second World War and endured some unbelievable hardships in the course of a long, forced march. Another man called Savvo who had some forty years service in the Works apart from the years between 1939 and 1945 when he was on active service. Like a lot of the old-timers in the Works, Savvo seemed to live entirely in the past. Ned was a big man from Norfolk and yours truly made up the fourth man on the yard team.

No matter what we might begin to discuss in the intervals between unloading wagons or lorries the talk would always in the end veer back to the "old days" and what it had been like to work under the strict supervision of the old time bowler hated foremen whose main object in life, it would appear, was to hound the workers under his care and make things as difficult as possible for them. The work was ten times harden then, old Savvo, would tell us with relish. Yes, that was the particular thing about it all, like most of his contemporaries he seemed to enjoy dwelling on the grisly details of their much-abused youth. There were no mechanical aids he would tell us - everything no matter how heavy, had to be manhandled and dragged about. Also there were any amount of petty restrictions and punishments, as for instance, the custom of "passing you out". This was not as you might reasonably imagine to someone walking by you but to the business of being suspended for a day for some real or imagined infringement of the rules. Thus, if a foreman was to come upon one of the men taking it easy, or maybe having a smoke when he should not be doing so, or even doing some particular job in the wrong way, he, the foreman, could immediately write you out a pass and send you home as a punishment. The loss of two or three day's pay was something not to be incurred too lightly, but from the frequency of the passing out it would seem that a lot of the old-timers delighted in depriving the men under their charge of the badly needed few shillings. The war changed all this like so much else and Savvo would dwell unbelievingly on the great changes he found when he came back in 1945. Especially the free and easy atmosphere, the independence of the workers and the reduced power of the foreman. But instead of rejoicing in all this as you might reasonably suppose he would, old Savvo would actually be incensed at the new freedom the men enjoyed. "The slackness, Pat, you just couldn't believe it, everything had gone to hell, no discipline or responsibility at all, everyone just doing as they pleased. Cor, I'll bet some of the real old timers would turn in their graves if they could have come back and seen it." But I suppose this is only the quirkiness of human nature and I have seen the same thing among old-time building and civil engineering workers who begrudged the comparative easy life to the younger generation who had never known what the sheer brutal exploitation of the 'twenties and the 'thirties' was like. I knew an old man who worked on the Shannon Electricity Scheme in Ireland more than forty years ago and he would grow quite choleric comparing the savage conditions on that particular job with the benefits of today's mechanisation in the industry. They almost all managed to give you the impression that they hankered after those times and would like to see them back again.

"Sweat, Pat?" he would deride. "You blokes don't know nothing about sweat. We didn't sweat back in the 'twenties, Pat, we sweated blood!" "More bleddy fool you," replied Ned the young Norfolkman with a yawn which only added to the fuel of poor Savvo's resentment.

Men like this feel cheated, perhaps, or just plain aggrieved that a younger and softer breed of men should have been spared the hardships and injustices of their own youth. But if the truth were known they wouldn't return to those times for love nor money - and wisely so. Yet they almost all managed to give the impression that they hankered after those times and would like to see them back again. Old Savvo, at any rate, used to grow positively nostalgic as he recounted his experiences in the din and suffocating heat of the smithy, which was the hardest department in the Works. ID X-MCMLXXV

There was a fine spacious canteen in the Works and in the winter months I would spend the dinner hour there every day, reading or perhaps jotting down a few notes. To get to the canteen you had to go out of the main gates, which were then closed and not reopened until shortly before it was time to clock back on again for the afternoon stint. Most of the men spent the hour in the canteen, a few went across to the Engineers or the Railwayman, where they could eat their sandwiches with a pint of ale, unlike a lot of these modern pubs where you'd be in danger of instant and not-too gentle eviction if you produced your own food. In the winter months I used the canteen a lot and read or took notes during the hour dinner break. One day, as I was sitting down to a book, one of the old-timers tapped me apologetically and asked if I'd mind giving him my place. "You see, mate," he explained, "I've sat there every working day for nigh on forty years, it's always been my place and if I had to sit anywhere else I'd feel sort of out of joint, you know, sort of put out." Yes, by no means, I hastened to assure him, he could have his seat if that's what he wanted. I quite understood, I told him, though it would have been more truthful to say that I pitied him for having got into such a terrible rut. For having allowed himself to have become such a slave to habit. He thanked me profusely and over the next half hour or so he gave me a detailed account of his life in the Works. A life of singular uneventfulness it seemed to me. Then at about five minutes past one he excused himself, saying that at this time everyday he took a nap for 20 minutes so that he could be refreshed and eager for his afternoon's work. This man was exceptional, to be sure, and there were a great many like him in the Works. I thought of him sitting in the same place day after working day, taking the same 20 minutes' snooze and setting off happily to clock on again until it was time to go home. I couldn't help wondering if that kind of contentment was a good thing. It seemed to me that my own life was becoming altogether too repetitive. Catching the early morning, clocking on and off four times a day and then arriving back in the same Northampton station every evening. I had visions of this sort of thing going on until it was time for me to retire. Discontentment began to set in.

I suppose you could go on for ever in a job or situation if it was just on a day-to-day or week-to-week basis, but once the notion occurred to you that you would never do anything else the position would become intolerable. That was how I saw it at any rate. It began to seem to me that my life was already over and before long I realised that I would have to pack up the job and find something else. Just to break the monotony of the routine, I believed, would be a tonic. I mentioned this to Jerry and Savvo one day as we had a pause between unloading wagons. Jerry guffawed his amusement. "Bloody routine, Pat, you don't know how lucky you are to have routine. I've seen times when I'd have given anything for ordinary routine, when you had some big bloomin Fritzie kicking you up the arse a dozen times a day and nothing in your belly for the past forty-eight hours, maybe."

There was no comparison at all, I argued, but nevertheless the monotony of the thing was getting me down and I intended to jack up this job. "Pat's right," the young Norfolkman put in, "it does get a bit monotonous here. I wouldn't mind looking around for another job myself."

"Naw, you don't want to do that, Ned," old Savvo advised, tongue in cheek. "You'll never make a success of your life if you keep jumping from job to job."

Ned looked at Savvo suspiciously, for he came in for a great deal of ribbing most of the time.

"Quite right," Jerry said with a snigger, "you'll never advance yourself and get a position of trust if you don't stay long enough in the same employment."

"Don't want a position of trust, do I?" Ned retorted. "All I want is the sodden week's wages and if it wasn't for that I wouldn't come to work at all."

"So you're only interested in the money?" Jerry said, aghast.

"You men, you don't take no pride in your work?"

"What's there to take pride in?" Ned wanted to know. "Emptying lorries and wagons? Dragging bogeys about? I don't see anything to take pride in there, do you?"

"Anything worth doing is worth doing well," old Savvo said solemnly. "You wouldn't have lasted two days here in the old days, Ned. You couldn't have stuck the pace."

And so we were back to the old days again. There was a consciousness of the bad old days before the war, which seemed to haunt everyone over the age of fifty in the Works. I think that decided me as much as anything else for just then I had a horrible vision of ending up like old Savvo - endlessly reminiscing about the job - which you might rightly accuse me of doing in this story about the Works!

ID X1-MCMLXXV

Chapter Fourteen

SWEENEY

"Get up, Sween! It's a quarter to, gone."

"I'd leave him," grumbled Mahon over by the door. "I'd leave him to hell. He was lively enough at one o'clock this morning - the Valley of Knockanure at the top of his bleddy voice. I own to Christ there's digs he'd be slaughtered in."

Sweeney blinked, unwilling to believe that it was morning already. It seemed only seconds since he had rolled into bed, surrendering to the half-sick, hobby-horse sensation of drifting away into blackness. His drunken sleep had done nothing for him at all.

"Sweeney, you toe-rag, get out of it! There's no singin' this morning."

"Oh, leave me, Spud, for God's sake," he moaned.

"Leave him surely." Mahon said, going out of the room.

"I'm damned if I'd call him."

His head filled with a vast, pulsating ache and queasiness strained, like a leashed dog, in the pit of his stomach; sleep was his best bet now, his one chance of appeasing the hangover. He closed his eyes, shutting out the sour-smelling room with its soiled and mottled paper, its close-packed single beds ranged side by side like grave-mounds, its chipped enamel bucket of stale, oily pee. Drowsiness lapped round him like sunwarmed waves and he smiled slyly, fancying that he had gulled Murphy into believing that he would follow them down. His breathing grew deeper as sleep encroached, lulling consciousness. He began to snore. And then he was jolted into cold wakefulness by the realisation that he would have to get up for his work; he must be still drunk to have imagined he could lie on today.

A quarter to seven gone! Groaning, he eased himself out from the warm clothes to sit, shivering, on the edge of the bed; after a moment he began dressing with stiff, puppet movements, hoping to check the lurking nausea and the malignant, burgeoning pain in his head. But then he had to lower himself gingerly on one knee to grope beneath his bed for a missing boot. The effort made his stomach heave and his head throbbed viciously. With clumsy, shaking fingers he half-laced the boots and then, averting his face from the bucket, he went out of the room.

Down in the dining room he tried not to look at the pale yolked egg and obscene shrunken sausage on the plate before him while he drank two cups of the weak, lodging-house tea in quick, measured sips. His fellow lodgers had all left the house now and the landlady had put his breakfast on the table when she was laying out theirs; he could eat it or not as he pleased. Obligation discharged, the rip would be back in bed now, snug and warm; the house was quiet except for the faint sound of traffic outside on the street. From the wall above the 'contemporary' sideboard opposite him the coronation portrait of Queen Elizabeth II regarded Sweeney with a blend of commiseration and contempt. He started to grimace back at it but the small effort made his headache worse and he subsided, praying the pain would ease. The hour of seven boomed funereally from the high clock in the hall, reminding him that he had barely half an hour to get to the site on the other end of the town. He got up from the table and went out of the house.

The bus stop was only a few doors away but there were two people in front of Sweeney and he cursed himself for not getting out a little sooner. The number seven was usually full at this stage and it would be just like one of the baluba conductors to bar him with an authoritative wave of a pink-palmed hand. But there were empty seats when the bus came and the conductor was a raw-looking culchie who would not have cared if they rode on the roof; Sweeney sat near the door where he hoped that the draught would help him recover and arrived at the stop outside the building site a minute or two before half-past seven. He clocked his card as the klaxon began its raucous wail and went to fetch his shovel from under the sheet of tarpaulin behind the cement shed.

Already the mixer drum was turning with a grating and a rasping that tore at his nerves and Bronteski, the Pole, was stacking sacks of cement conveniently close to the hopper. They ignored each other, and Sweeney spat dryly on his calloused hands and prayed Jesus to make the morning pass quickly. Six o'clock was an eternity away, too awful to think of. He began scooping gravel into the hopper with short, powerful strokes but almost at once he was leaning on the T-handled shovel, forehead clammy with cold, sick sweat, his stomach heaving dangerously. He stayed bent for a minute, weathering the bout, and then he looked up to find the cold alien eyes of the Pole on him. Bronteski would have it in the nose for him over last night but that was the very least of his worries now. Later on, when he felt more himself, with the help of God, he'd get back at the cow-faced bohunk. The Pole pulled the lever and the hopper rose, creaking and screeching under its load, and when all but a residue of the mix had gone into the rasping drum, he jerked the lever sharply so that the hopper banged itself clean. The noise hammered on Sweeney's brain, making him gasp with pain. He closed his eyes as the hopper descended and then he began shovelling again.

Bad scran to the Erris men anyway - but for them he wouldn't be in this state. With only Bronteski for company he wouldn't have drunk more than four or five pints in the Wheatsheaf on his way home from work. It was a penance being with Bronteski after even the second pint when he started in on his tale of woe about the war and Dachau and all the rest of it and began taking out faded pictures of himself in uniform and of his wife - a blonde, stolidly handsome girl whom he hadn't seen in all of twenty years. They were at that stage when he spotted the Geraghty brothers and Hughie McAndrew throwing darts in the smoke-room and, in desperation he had called in to them. The Erris men left off the darts and came through at once, eager for news of what had been happening in town since they left for Lincolnshire and the farmers early in the summer.

Bronteski, left out in the cold, had gone away in a huff and from there on until closing time it had been pints of light and bitter as fast as the landlord could pull. Afterwards in the Greek's cafe, and later in the gent's on the market square, they had polished off a five-noggin bottle of Scotch between them and Sweeney had performed a snake dance in the alley behind All Saints' before an envious-looking policeman had wearily moved them on. The Errismen and their beet-money! They'd be expecting him in the Wheatsheaf again tonight but, by Christ, they'd have a wait.

Halfway through the fourth or fifth mix Sweeney had to stop shovelling again. Hunched over the shovel, head down, he was tempted to chuck the work for today, to make some excuse at the pay-hut and go back to the digs. No-one as sick as he was should have to give ten hours mullacking sand and ballast; it wasn't human to ask it. But some small store of pride kept him where he was and mercifully, at last, the whistle blew for the morning break. Sweeney went slowly to the mess-hut and drank a mug of hot, sweet tea sitting unspeaking in a corner. Some time, about mid-morning he began to feel better. The craw-sickness left him first and then the headache. He felt weak and washed-out now, the strength seemed to have left his arms and he found himself looking forward more and more to the brief respite which the raising of each hopperfull gave him. Bronteski could have lent a hand with nothing to do but operate the mixer and throw in the cement but no, he'd sulk all day now like a bear with a sore bum. Well, let him; there would be "again" in it as the Erris men said.

Sweeney was hungry by dinner-time and he ate two thick bacon sandwiches along with another mug of tea. Then, ignoring the hubbub of voices around him, he put his head on his arms and dozed for the remainder of the half-hour break. He awoke to the scraping of forms against the rough concrete floor as the men started leaving the hut; another five hours to go - God, what he'd give to be able to crawl away and sleep in some corner for the afternoon. But he felt better when he went out in the air and, leering at the Pole, he moistened his hands with spittle and began filling the hopper again. Bronteski split and emptied a bag of cement over the sand and ballast and, be cause the wind had changed, the grey dust drifted across to Sweeney, settling on his face and hair.

"That's it - scatter the flamin' thing!" he yelled, glad of the excuse to quarrel with the Pole. Bronteski shrugged but next time he was more careful and soon Sweeney was too happy in his returning well being to want to argue more. He worked with a steady rhythm, a mindless, regular movement that would see him through the rest of the day. The noise of the mixer came to him as a muted rumbling, an unobtrusive theme-tune, and the swish of his shovel, as he sliced through the gravel, reassured him with the proof of his own strength. There were not many men about these days could feed a mixer single-handed - moreover after a night like he'd had on the booze. He felt only contempt for Bronteski, clinging to his cushy job. But dammit, he had a bit of brain, too, hadn't he, and it was time he took stock of himself. How often had he come to work like this, sick and suffering, cursing himself for ten kinds of a fool? He was over thirty now with ten years of hard graft on building sites all over England behind him and nothing to show for it beyond his yearly run home and two Burton-made suits back in the digs. He didn't gamble, he didn't smoke and his rare, drunken encounters with women picked up in the pubs accounted for only a fraction of the money he spent. If only he could cut down on the beer! But it wasn't just the beer, either; it was company. He always seemed to meet up with someone.

But there was an answer to that too, if a man put his mind to it. Shun the pubs altogether, that was the trick. The money he was earning - he could save a tenner a week if he wished and be comfortably off in no time at all. Get to hell out of John Bull's country and go home with enough saved to give him a proper start in life. A little sweet-and-tobacco shop, maybe - that shouldn't cost too much - or door-to-door deliveries of coal and sticks. There must be dozens of openings for a man with a bit of "go" and initiative - and capital. You'd get nowhere at all without the old bank balance. The idea took hold of Sweeney, making him tremble with excitement. God! but it would be grand to be living in your own home town again, among your own sort, known and respected. He'd be Tom to people again, not Sween, not Sweeney as he was here or worse still, Pat; and if he had his own yard or counter to lean on he'd be Mister Sweeney to business friends and travellers. It would be nice to be somebody for a change; here he was nothing at all, a nobody, a buck-navvy restricted to the company of illiterates like his mates of the night before.

The hopper was empty again and, chuckling with exultation he sent sand and gravel flying before him until it towered above the gauge-line, a mountain in miniature. Magnanimously he winked at the Pole; the poor exiled bastard , who could be hard on him? Bronteski stared back at him, a look of slight puzzlement on his broad face, and then he tugged angrily at the lever as though piqued at Sweeney's good form.

"Cheer up, Bonnie boy, you only live once!" Sweeney yelled.

He'd thaw the Pole out in spite of himself; life was too short for hard feelings. Almost unable to contain the joy that welled up inside him, Sweeney worked like mad, the shovel light as a broom in his hands.

He had almost forgotten what it was like to live at home, to belong to a community, to have roots. But all that could be his again if he just had the guts to bring it about. Look at the chap of the Brannigans from Patrick Street - six years in the States only and back home now secure for life with his fish-and-chip saloon, his own boss, a man of substance in the town. Well, Tom Sweeney has as much gumption as Packy Brannigan any day and with the help of God he'd prove it. He'd put one ten-pound note by every blessed week from now, beginning next pay day. Five hundred a year, a thousand in two, two thousand quid in four years - a tidy little nest-egg in any man's language. It would mean cutting the beer out completely, of course - cold turkey as they said in the films - but that was the only way. Half- measures for him would be fatal. It would call for pucks of determination but he could do it if he never lost sight of his goal. He'd have a couple of early nights a week, kill another night or two at the Picturedrome or the Plaza, buy a few cheap books from the barrowboys on the market each Saturday - that way he'd take a lot of the sting out of being on the tack. And then (time flew when you had something to work for) in no time at all he'd be back home again, reliving the life he had loved.

The Sundays he remembered with such longing! the secret, conspirators' knock that got you in at the side door, the pints drunk in an aura of close fellowship behind shuttered windows; droning, whispered talk and shaded light, thick whorls of tobacco smoke wreathing laxly above them. The late dinner with bacon that tasted like bacon and green cabbage you could smell from the head of the street, spuds breaking flowerily at the touch of the fork. And afterwards the excitement of the game beyond in the Park, itself only a prelude to another session in pubs allowed open for the match, among loud-voiced countrymen with cycle-pumps protruding from their jackets, and raincoats strapped in, bandoleer fashion, over broad shoulders. He remembered the Sunday the Widow Morissey had recognised himself and Clancy for townies - non bona fides - and ordered them out of her house. Clancy had called her a Turk to the sly delight of the Muckalee men and they had to skip off down to Langton's before the Garda on duty outside could answer the widow's outraged cries.

Ten years away from it all and old friends and faces growing fewer with each visit home; he was a fool to have stayed so long in a land as alien to him, almost, as it must be to that poor unfortunate Pole. Life was too short to be spent among strangers, unknown and unknowing; in another ten or fifteen years he'd begin to feel his age and from then on it would be a slow decline until he ended up like one of those poor, broken-down Paddies who come begging at presbytery doors on Sunday. It was up to him now, he would make a little niche for himself in his native town and live like a civilised being or he could stay here and rot. Willpower could do it.

Round about four o'clock a ten-ton lorry backed in with a fresh load of gravel and Sweeney got the driver to tip up as close as he could without impeding the rise of the hopper; the gravel was new-washed and heavy but, full of his dream, Sweeney resumed shovelling, excitement lending power to his arm. Stroke after stroke, he dug into the glistening ballast before attacking the softer, heavier sand. The sand heap sank under the repeated thrusts of the shovel, collapsing in a series of tiny landslides, and the crown of gravel began perceptibly to lower. Bronteski had run out of cement now and was frantically signalling the dumper driver to come and fetch him some more. "Come on Bronnie, I'll give you a lift," Sweeney said, but his earlier mood of good fellowship was beginning to wear thin. He felt a certain irritation - with him the first signs of weariness. Another hour and a half to go; well, he was over the worst of it and once they were into the last hour he'd endure anything. Home, James, then - straight home. He'd face the other way when the bus passed the Wheatsheaf. Mahon and the others would have nothing to crib about tonight - not on his account anyway. Just let him get the next hour over and all would be well. But the next hour was the worst since dinner-break because there was a panic that the oversight they were concreting would not be completed in time and a second dumper was put on to speed up the work. Bronteski, with a great show of comradeship, found himself a shovel and began helping Sweeney to load the hopper. But the help was out-weighed by the fact of the second dumper and Sweeney's back and arms began to ache with exhaustion. The strength seemed to be draining out of him and once, when he straightened, a swarm of tiny floating flecks appeared before his eyes. The shirt clung to his skin now and his trouser legs lay clammy against his thighs. And then his headache came back, cruelly insistent though pitched in a lower key. His tongue had gone dry as a paper and his mouth had a bad taste. At ten to six the ganger in charge sent word back that they had too much concrete mixed now: they might dump the mix they had in the drum and cover up what remained in the hopper so that it would be fit to use tomorrow. Sweeney cursed their bungling and made his way stiffly to hide his shovel beneath the sheet of tarpaulin at the rear of the cement shed. He hoped it would find him in better shape tomorrow, for, Mother of God; he'd have to have one more drink. He hung about until the klaxon sounded at a minute to six and then he clocked his card and went out the gate. He was at the bus-stop, waiting for the number seven when Bronteski joined him; neither of them spoke for a moment and then Bronteski made a sign, his broad Polish face framing a question.

"Yes," said Sweeney, "I suppose 'tis as well for us."

"Ve go Wheatsheaf," said Bronteski, and smiled his slow, melancholy, Slav smile.

ID X11-MCMLXXV

Chapter Fifteen

DÓNALL PEADAR MAC AMHLAIGH

Rugadh Dónall Mac Amhlaigh i nGaillimh i 1926. D'aistrigh a mhuintir go Cill Cainnigh nuair a bhí Dónall 13 bhliain d'aois. I ndiaidh dó an gnáth-bhunoideachas fháil bhí sé, dála go leor eile, gan phost agus chuaigh sé isteach in Arm na hÉireann. Nuair a fuarthas amach go raibh Gaeilge líofa aige cuireadh sa Chéad Chath Gaelach é. Ba ansin a d'fhoghlaim sé an meas a bhí aige ar chultúr na haicme oibre agus a thuiscint do shaol na hÉireann - saol a bhí ag athrú, mar a léirigh meath na Gaeilge. B'in an t-am a thosaigh luachanna gallda an mhargaidh ag dul i gceann ar shaol na tuaithe in Éirinn.

Bhíodh sé ag tagairt de shíor do na laethe úd sa Chéad Chath mar laethe a mbíodh buncheisteanna, gach uile 'tuige' agus 'cèn chaoi', á bplé trí Ghaeilge.

Bhí súil le rath ag Dónall nuair a D'fhág sé an tArm, ach ba ghearr go raibh sé ar an mbád bán agus bhain sé Northampton amach i 1951 le glacadh le post cónaithe mar ghiolla ospidéil san ospidéal áitiúil. Ba sheoda i gcultúr aicme oibre a linne a scéalta sna luathsheascaidí faoi Mhátrúin agus faoi "mhopanna". Agus is ceacht i gcomhaireachtáil ilchultúrtha a scéal faoin *Uasal M'Baka*, an chéad dochtúir den chine gorm i Northampton.

Nuair a ghluais sé ar ball isteach i dtithe lóistín, cuireadh ábhar do scéalta a bhainfeadh le seomraí á roinnt, dinnéir shuaracha agus nmá lóistín leathchraiceáilte ar fáil dó - scéalta a mbíodh léamh san *Irish Democrat* sa Bhreatain, in Ireland's Own in Éirinn, gan trácht ar *Inniu, Anois,* an *Irish Post* agus an *Irish Times* etc. Ba scéalta iad seo a léigh muid ar fad - ár saol féin a bhí faoi thrácht iontu - coinníollacha a raibh cur amach againn orthu, na mná céanna lóistín.

B'é a fhearacht chéanna é ag na hoibrithe tógála. D'oibrigh Dónall ar gach príomhláthair thógála in Oirthear Lár na Breataine. Ó Mhilton Kegnes go Coventry, ón M.1 go dtí an M.6. Patrick MacGill comhaimseartha ab ea é agus taifead á dhéanamh aige ar anó, ar chrá agus ar lúcháir a chomhleacaithe. Thug a léiriú ar chomrádaíocht ar na láthracha tógála misneach don té a bhí beaguchtach. Mhúscail a chur síos ar an ngaingear spídiúil sanntach a mbíodh hata mór á chaitheamh aige (toisc cloigeann bheag a bheith aige) cuimhní dóite iontu siúd a thuig na coinníollacha seo, agus chinntigh sé a n-áiteanna sa stair dá leithéid.

Rinneamar uile iontas dá chur síos ar charactair, ar láthracha tógála agus ar phubanna in *Dialann Deoraí*, foilsithe níos faide anonn i mBéarla faoin teideal *The Irish Navvy*. Arís arais, is cuid de stair ár linne é go mbíodh geaingers ag earcú do Murphy agus ag dáileadh luach saothar amach i dtithe tabhairne. Bhí siad uile nochtaithe os comhair an tsaoil i leabhair Dhónall, i nGaeilge agus i mBéarla. Tugadh míniú glé ar an meabhair agus na matáin a ndearnadh dúshaothrú orthu chun na mótarbhealaí M agus Fothalmhán Londain a thógáil. Agus faoin scéal seo uile bhí crá croí an deoraí. Níor ghabhadh buíochas riamh as cabhrú chun an Bhreatain a thógáil.

I Northampton ba bhunaitheoir de chuid an *Northern Ireland Civil Rights Association* é Dónall MacAmhlaigh a thug ar bhunadh na háite a machnamh a dhéanamh, sna 70 óidí ar a laghad, ar a raibh idir lámha ag na bunchreidmhigh Phrotastúnacha i d'Tuaisceart Éireann.

Níos faide anonn ba bhall gníomhach de chuid an *Northampton Connolly Association* agus ár múinteoir deonach Gaeilge é ar feadh dhá bhliana sa Lárionad Dífhostaíochta. Bhíodh idir 12 agus 20 duine ag freastal ar na rangacha seo, iad idir 8 agus 50 bliain d'aois, agus thug Dónall bunghreim ar theanga ár sinsir dúinn. B'in a bhí uainn le tús a chur le teacht ar ár bhféiniúlacht. Ba ghníomh dearbhtha é agus d'oibrigh sé.

Scáthánú a dhéanamh ar an saol, ina shimplíocht, ina neamhurchóid agus ina chruatan - b'in neart Dhónaill. Bhí acmhainní simplí aige agus bhíodh a bhreithiúnais thaifeadta fírinneach agus macánta riamh.

Le déanaí thugadh sé an-ghean dá rothar. Rothar speisialta a d'ordaigh sé go speisialta, an saghas a chleachtaíodh na Gardaí, gléasanna móra millteacha ar nós tancanna Centurion. Ba mhinic é le feiceáil ag rothaíocht ar fud an bhaile, luas rialta faoi. Mar a tharlaíonn, d'úsáid sé an rothar céanna an lá a d'imigh sé uainn.

Níor bhain polaitíocht Dhónall go díreach le polaitíocht aos teoirice an Mharxachais. Bhí a chuid fealsúnachta bunaithe ar chúinse simplí loighciúil, go raibh Iarthar na hEorpa saibhir agus go raibh an móramh á dhúshaothrú ag an mionlach. Ba ar bhonn morálta a bhunaigh sé a bhreithiúnais, cuid dá oidhreacht agus dá thógáil Chaitliceach, b'fhéidir. D'aithin sé croí na héagóra, an módh go gcuirtear muid uile ag obair in aghaidh a chéile.

Beidh cuimhne againn ar Dhónall de bharr a dhaonnachta, a mhacántachta agus a shimplíochta. A chur síos ar dheacrachtaí blainta tosaigh a dheoraíocht, thuigeamar é agus b'as taithí a tháinig an tuiscint seo. Ba duine dinn féin é agus chuir sé ár mothúcháin in iúl. Tá ár múinteoir caillte againn ach is láidre an chúis dá bharr agus mairfidh sí.

Peadar O'Maólagain,
Rúnaí
Northampton Connolly Association
Comhar 111-MCMLXXX1X

Always.

Forever.